For more than forty years,
Yearling has been the leading name
in classic and award-winning literature
for young readers.

Yearling books feature children's
favorite authors and characters,
providing dynamic stories of adventure,
humor, history, mystery, and fantasy.

Trust Yearling paperbacks to entertain,
inspire, and promote the love of reading
in all children.

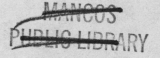

# The Orange Trees of Versailles

❖

*Annie Pietri*

Translated from the French by
Catherine Temerson

A YEARLING BOOK

Published by
Yearling
an imprint of
Random House Children's Books
a division of Random House, Inc.
New York

Originally published in France in 2000 by Bayard Editions Jeunesse

Visit us on the Web! www.randomhouse.com/kids

Educators and librarians, for a variety of teaching tools, visit us at
www.randomhouse.com/teachers

ISBN: 0-440-41948-4

Reprinted by arrangement with Delacorte Press

Printed in the United States of America

November 2005

10 9 8 7 6 5 4 3 2 1

OPM

# The Orange Trees of Versailles

## ❦ 1 ❧

"**A**ntoine, your daughter is going on fourteen and she's still not working. At her age, my children had already been earning their keep for a long time. Surely you're not planning on feeding Marion until her wedding day?"

Augustine Lebon, Gaspard Lebon's wife, was speaking. She stood in front of Antoine Dutilleul, arms akimbo, her large reddish hands on her hips, as she continued.

"I hear that the king's favorite, the Marquise de Montespan, is looking for servants. This may be an opportunity for Marion to become part of the domestic staff. Your daughter would see the king every day! Gaspard and I feel that your Marion is a very capable girl, and so do all the other people who work in the gardens. Just think! A gardener's daughter who knows how to read and write! You're a good father, but you shouldn't let her run around the grounds dressed like a boy, weeding the garden."

Antoine looked straight into Augustine's eyes. "She's not weeding the garden. She's collecting plants!"

1

## 2

Though Antoine wasn't one to be browbeaten, that morning he introduced his daughter to the marquise. As soon as they walked into the small drawing room, he began playing with his hat, squeezing it in his rough brown hands. He was amazed. Athénaïs de Montespan, the beautiful marquise, had decided to personally choose a servant from among the seven girls who were waiting in the pantry.

Marion was the first to appear before her. The favorite scrutinized the girl with her light blue eyes—the same eyes whose bright gaze captivated the king and fascinated the entire court. Yet the marquise was not liked at Versailles. Her reputation was that of an unscrupulous schemer, an ambitious courtesan who would do anything to remain in the king's favor. Marion had already seen her on the grounds during the king's walks, so she knew the marquise was very beautiful.

On this day, as she received her visitors, the marquise was seated in a large armchair, surrounded by the blue and gold fabric of her splendid dress. She was wearing the king's colors. Her lovely blond locks framed her face becomingly.

At her every gesture a magnificent perfume filled the air. Indeed, everything around her was magnificent—the Venetian mirrors, the gilded paneling, the refined tapestries and drapery, the Oriental silk carpets, and the crystal chandeliers reflecting the golden blaze of the candles.

Marion felt intimidated, no less so than if she were being introduced to the queen. Though Athénaïs wasn't the queen of France, she was all-powerful. She was married to the Marquis of Montespan, but she held full sway over Louis XIV's heart; she had been his favorite for seven years and had already given him three children.

"Your daughter looks frail, Antoine Dutilleul. You've lied about her age."

"I didn't lie, Madame la Marquise."

Athénaïs did not look reassured. "Let's not misunderstand each other," she said. "I don't want servants who are too young and whom my children might mistake for playmates. My little darlings might become foolishly attached, as the king did to the children of his mother's chambermaid. Your little girl looks like she's ten or eleven. Are you sure she'll be strong enough to work in my service?"

"I'm certain of it," said Antoine. "When my wife, Marie, died, Marion wasn't even ten. She misses her mother and has trouble sleeping. She can sleep no more than an hour or two at a time. But she's a hard worker and she never tires. She has to keep busy all the time, even at night. It interferes with my own sleep. Not to mention the cost in candles!"

Athénaïs's eyes lit up and she smiled fleetingly, revealing her perfect teeth. Encouraged, Antoine stepped closer to her, and with a backward glance at his daughter, he whispered: "Her favorite occupation is making sachets with the flowers she gathers on the grounds. Last year I wanted to apprentice her to a perfumer, but they'll only take boys. Yet she knows the scent of every plant and every flower and has an incredible memory. I've never seen anything like it. She could be a gardener, too, but that's certainly not a girl's profession!"

This child, with her beautiful dark eyes and wise, gentle gaze, disconcerted the marquise. She was unlike any of the girls who had formerly served her so badly and whom she had mercilessly dismissed.

Marion had a long, pale face; a straight, undistinguished nose; messy blond hair gathered under a coarse cotton bonnet; and a skinny, almost ungainly body. Her dress was too short and her clogs were slightly too big. Nonetheless, the marquise found herself responding to the girl's indefinable charm. Well accustomed to every kind of court intrigue, the favorite was a good judge of character. Everything set her apart from this girl—nobility, beauty, wealth, and power. Yet, just looking at Marion stirred a strange feeling within her: a kind of awe tinged with anxiety. She sensed that the girl had a strong mind and unusual determination.

Leaning toward her lady-in-waiting and confidante, Claude des Œillets, the marquise made her choice. All the girls waiting in the pantry were dismissed.

"Your daughter will start working for me right away," said Athénaïs. "I only hope everything you said is true. If not, she'll be sent away like the others."

Marion lowered her head to hide her feelings. She didn't want to be parted from her father and had se cretly hoped the marquise would dismiss them both. Her eyes shone with tears when Antoine hugged her and said goodbye.

Marion followed a servant girl down the corridors and up the back stairways. Their steps echoed on the red floor tiles, fragrant from fresh wax. The servants' small bedrooms were located on the top floor, under the roof. Each was shared by two people. The room she was shown was already occupied, for clothes were strewn on one of the two beds. A tiny table was covered with toilet articles, soiled plates, and bread crumbs. The solitary skylight window, through which a slice of dark gray sky could be seen, filtered a dim light into the room. The entire floor smelled of dust and humidity, mixed with the stench of urine from the chamber pots that had not yet been emptied.

Suddenly Marion saw a young girl running toward her.

"I'm Lucie, Lucie Cochois. We're going to be living

together, I see!" the girl said, smiling. "Follow me, dear. The marquise wants you in the formal drawing room immediately."

❧❧❧

Meanwhile, bowing awkwardly, Antoine left Athénaïs de Montespan's chambers. On his way to the orangery, he looked up at the sky and put his creased hat back on his head. A storm was brewing.

## ❧ 3 ❧

Since morning, thunder had pealed like drumrolls around the Château de Versailles. Heavy, windswept clouds gathered with incredible speed and hung over the slate roofs like a lead dome. For the month of June, the heat was oppressive. It was dark. The windows of the favorite's apartment overlooked the royal court-yard, which was bathed in a harsh, yellowish light. The marquise was sitting on a sofa, surrounded by several piles of soft, downy pillows, waiting for the storm. Nervously, she caressed her dog, a shaggy, slightly crazed breed of spaniel that answered to the name of Pyrrhos.

Suddenly, lightning struck near the stately courtyard gate. An enormous, beautiful ball of fire burst into a spray of light, like fireworks. Then a thunderclap, as loud as the boom of a cannon, broke through the static air of late afternoon. All the windowpanes of the château rattled. Pyrrhos scrambled under the couch and hid behind his mistress's skirts.

The marquise was afraid of storms. For her, the gates

of hell had opened. The demons of the underworld were crawling toward her, arms outstretched, eager to grasp her neck and choke her. They would soon be ripping out her heart with their monstrous claws. Lucifer was impatiently waiting for the sinister task to be completed; then he would suck her body into the boiling abyss of his entrails. . . .

The chambermaids rushed busily around Athénaïs, who had fainted. They gave her smelling salts, Hungarian water with its valuable perfume, and vinegar. They fanned her. In vain. The marquise remained unconscious. Beads of sweat formed on the milky skin of her bare neck and shoulders, gradually washing off the powder with which she was dusted every morning. On a small table, cinnamon-scented pastilles were smoldering in a china incense burner.

Marion had no idea why the marquise had wanted her by her side. She stood next to the couch obediently, silently watching a servant unlace the marquise's corset.

From his hiding place, Pyrrhos growled and bared his fangs whenever someone approached his mistress. He even tried to bite Lucie's ankle as she brought Madame de Montespan some holy water. Lucie responded by kicking him in the chops. Peevishly, the dog retreated under the couch again, squealing.

The thunder and lightning continued without respite well into the evening. Finally, it started to rain.

Marion liked storms. Since she wasn't needed, she walked to the window and admired the beautiful spectacle of the raging sky. From this second-floor window she could see the black-and-white-checkered pavement of the marble courtyard. Huge raindrops fell to the ground, spattering about, and soon everything was completely flooded. Water overflowed from the roofs, gushed out of the drainpipes, and streamed down the windowpanes.

~~~❧~~~

Claude des Œillets grabbed the marquise's arm and brought her back to her senses. When she regained consciousness, Athénaïs asked for Marion, who returned to the sofa.

The room was lit by dozens of candles. It was as bright as the sunniest hour of a summer day. The favorite was as afraid of the dark as she was of storms.

"The girl is here, madame," des Œillets announced.

"Tell her to come closer!"

Marion stood in front of the marquise, eyes lowered, expecting a reprimand for having moved away. But without saying anything, the marquise took her in her arms and hugged her for a long time. The other servants and maids walked off to tend to their affairs. Marion was puzzled, but she didn't dare move. Suddenly, Pyrrhos, whom everyone had forgotten since Lucie had kicked him, rushed out from under the couch in a mad fury. All these women constantly touching his adored mistress, and now this stranger being petted by her—it was all too much! Galvanized by the storm, fired up with rage and jealousy, the spaniel sank his fearsome teeth into Marion's right calf. Her cries of pain were drowned out by a thunderclap that was even louder than the previous ones. Athénaïs thought the demons of death were back on the rampage. And as Marion, whose leg was bleeding profusely, struggled to get away from both dog and mistress, the marquise hugged her ever more insistently.

Lucie ran to the small table, snatched the incense burner, and struck Pyrrhos on the head. The dog released Marion's leg and slid to the ground. An incandescent scented pastille dropped on his nose and burned it. Then the pastille fell to the carpet, leaving a black spot amid the bloodstains.

∽೦ᔛᗢ∾

The next morning, the weather was beautiful. The pastel glow of dawn shed a pink light on the gilded bronze garlands running the length of the slate rooftops. When Claude des OEillets told the marquise what had happened, Athénaïs was sitting up in her wide bed, enjoying a copious breakfast. She felt very sorry for her poor Pyrrhos with his bruised head, squinting eyes, and swollen red nose. To console him, she handed him a fistful of small pistachio macaroons, which he gobbled up.

After giving her orders for the day, the marquise glanced around her room.

Marion, her new servant, was not present to see her get out of bed; she was not in attendance for the court ceremony called the *lever*.

"Why did the dog bite me, Lucie? I didn't do anything to him!"

"He's a nasty creature! He bites everyone. Even the marquise!" Lucie explained. "She lets him sink his teeth into her pretty hands and just laughs. She claims he's being playful. You must always watch out for him when you get near her. He's as jealous as a tiger! Even the king is wary of him."

Exhausted from pain, Marion had slept much longer than usual. She had felt hot and then chilled to the bone. Lucie had sat by her bedside and nursed her. As soon as she'd seen her, Marion had instantly trusted this sixteen-year-old redhead. She was on the plump side, with kind green eyes and lots of freckles. In the two years that she had been working for the favorite, Lucie had managed to make everyone like her.

Marion wiped away the tears that were rolling down her cheeks.

"I wish I could see my father. I was so happy at

home!" Marion cried. "I'm confused by everything that happened last night. I don't understand it at all."

"The marquise is afraid of the devil," said Lucie. "She has a constant stream of astrologers and soothsayers who come to see her for a handsome fee. They tell her a lot of nonsense, and the terrible thing is, she believes it." Lucie lowered her voice. "One of the soothsayers is a real witch. She told the marquise she would die on a stormy night. So now the marquise is terribly afraid of storms. But try not to think about it anymore, Marion. Go back to sleep. I'm sure you'll get used to your new life very fast. We've all been through this."

Lucie took Marion in her arms. As she was being cradled, Marion clasped the little medallion of the Virgin Mary that hung around her neck. For four years she had been wearing it, ever since her mother's death. Marion missed her mother dreadfully. She shut her eyes and let her tears flow again.

❧❧❧

So that Marion could rest, Lucie worked for two. Four days later, her friend was better and could walk. She had suffered from her wound but also from her confinement in that dismal bedroom with low ceilings. She missed the open air and the beautiful trees in the gardens. To console her, Lucie went round to the kitchen repeatedly and brought her candied fruit or cake on the sly.

That evening, thanks to the young cook Martin

Taillepierre, Lucie selected some choice morsels from the dishes that had been brought back from the marquise's table.

"Looks as if Martin has a soft spot for you!" remarked Marion, untying the large dish towel their meal was wrapped in.

Lucie blushed to the tips of her ears. The two girls laughed as they gobbled down the white meat of fricasséed partridge, asparagus, a small pâté of pike, white bread, and half a jar of jam. It was a real feast.

"My, you have a good appetite! It warms the heart!" said Lucie. She drank a large glass of water and added, "Let's hurry. The marquise wants all her ladies by her side before retiring to bed. That's when she selects her busy girls."

"Busy girls?" asked Marion, puzzled.

"Get dressed and let's go. I'll explain on the way."

Marion took off the nightgown Lucie had lent her and slipped into her old dress. Her friend tied an apron around her waist. It was a gift. Though it wasn't new, it was clean and well ironed. Marion threw her arms around Lucie to thank her, kissing her loudly on each cheek. Then she gathered her hair up, adjusted her bonnet, and put on her clogs.

The formal quarters were bustling with familiar activity. Marion breathed in the smells wafting up from the kitchens and listened to the soft squeaking of the wooden floors, as well as the bursts of laughter coming from the valets in the interior courtyard below and the quarrels between the laundresses and the chambermaids in the linen room.

She had fully recovered. With every step, she felt her strength and love of life returning.

Just before they reached the door to Athénaïs de Montespan's bedroom, Lucie drew Marion aside.

"If you're chosen tonight—"

"Chosen to do what?" Marion interrupted, intrigued.

"To watch over the marquise's sleep," Lucie whispered. "She can't stand being alone, especially at night. Again, it's all because of the devilish nonsense the quack astrologers have crammed into her head! So she needs company. You spend the whole night in the bedroom, watching the candles and replacing them as soon as they die down. The marquise wants light and life around her in case she wakes up. And she wakes up often! One must never remain idle. So those of us who are selected discuss the latest court gossip, talk about our suitors, embroider, play, eat. In other words, we keep busy. But beware! One must never fall asleep under any circumstances." Lucie smiled at Marion. "It shouldn't be a problem for you. I've never seen anyone sleep so little. That's surely why you're as thin as a broomstick!"

At that moment, the other servants were beginning to enter Athénaïs's bedroom. Lucie and Marion joined them.

## 5

The favorite was pacing up and down her bedroom, brandishing a letter from Louis XIV like a trophy.

"Mesdemoiselles, the king is in Fontainebleau!" announced the marquise. "He'll be returning to Versailles tomorrow morning. And in honor of the victory of his armies in Franche-Comté, His Majesty will be throwing a celebration whose splendor will surpass anything we've ever seen. There will be six days of festivities in the course of the two summer months. The first is scheduled for July fourth. So you can see we have very little time to get ready! Mademoiselle des Œillets, see to it that the tailor and seamstresses get here first thing in the morning."

The servants and chambermaids, at first bewildered by all this news, started to whisper among themselves, and gradually their delight became apparent. Marion squeezed Lucie's hand very tightly. She had a clear recollection of the royal entertainment of 1668, which she had witnessed—true, from a distance—with her mother and father. This time, she would be seeing the fête from a much closer vantage point. Being in the service of Montespan, she would surely be privy to all the little secret preparations—and she was glad of it.

This evening Athénaïs was wearing a white silk nightdress that swirled around her, gently swishing with her every move, and high-heeled mules trimmed with swan feathers. Her soft, azure velvet dressing gown set off the golden streaks in her flowing hair.

Even without makeup, Marion found her breathtaking.

After launching into a monologue in praise of the conqueror king, extolling his skill and valor in battle, the marquise concluded by asserting loudly and clearly that Louis XIV was without doubt the greatest king in all the world.

It was nearly midnight when she decided to go to bed. Pyrrhos, who had been sniffing the chambermaids' dresses and growling, immediately jumped on the bed to be next to her. Finally, the favorite called Claude des Œillets and whispered in her ear.

"The girl in clogs, by herself. Oh, and summon my astrologer, too, for tomorrow morning, ten o'clock."

The lady-in-waiting went up to the servants, who were now holding back yawns.

"You're the one who's staying, Marion," she announced, directing her icy stare at the other girls. "Alone."

Lucie winked at her friend and vanished.

The marquise was propped up on her pillows with

Pyrrhos at her feet. As the other girls left, des Œillets gave orders that they bring in a light meal. Marion felt tiny and miserable in that bedroom, for without its usual bustle it suddenly seemed huge and awesomely luxurious. Athénaïs had exquisite taste, and the king was very generous. Everything here was expensive. At this late hour, in the empty space and silence, the true value of every little thing stood out.

Marion didn't dare move or speak. Finally, Claude des Œillets signaled to her to come closer. To the girl's great disappointment, the lady-in-waiting added nothing to what Lucie had said. She merely stressed the fact that Marion must not fall asleep under any circumstances.

"The night meal will be sent up from the kitchens very soon," the lady-in-waiting said. "You can help yourself to whatever you want. But be careful. If you overeat—and you're not used to it—you'll doze off. Don't forget you'll be all alone until morning. There'll be no one here to shake you awake!"

"I won't fall asleep, madame. I'm used to staying up."

"That's what they all say," des Œillets retorted. "I might as well warn you. The job is easy to land but hard to keep."

"I know I won't sleep, madame."

"You conceited little girl! We'll see about this tomorrow."

Marion went to sit on a stool the lady-in-waiting showed her with a vague gesture. In front of her, on a console, was a needlepoint canvas another girl must have started during a long night of wakefulness. The work was uneven and the skeins were all tangled up, as though a kitten had played with them. The whole mess suggested a fierce struggle against sleep. Marion began untangling the threads; she would work on the needlepoint later.

Soon the meal arrived on a little table. Two valets set it down in front of her.

Marion stared wide-eyed at the tempting roast chicken, the pie filled with hard-boiled eggs, the compote, the fruit jelly, and the pitcher of orgeat milk.

"Two feasts in one night!" Marion said under her breath. "Madame des Œillets is right. I'll certainly fall asleep over that confounded needlework if I eat."

So she didn't. Instead, she changed three candles that were almost spent. Then she once again settled onto the stool, cursing the dozens of knots in the masses of thread that had to be disentangled.

Seconds later she gave a start. The curtains around the canopy bed, which had been drawn to give the marquise her privacy, suddenly parted. To her great astonishment, Marion saw Athénaïs get up, slip on her mules, and, with Pyrrhos at her heels, go over to a small, very beautiful inlaid cabinet. The marquise took out a pretty box of varnished wood and then walked toward Marion, who immediately stood up and made a quick curtsey.

"Open this box," the marquise ordered. "If what your

father said is true, you've got better things to do than that ridiculous needlepoint." She placed the box on the console.

Slowly, Marion went nearer. Athénaïs studied her closely.

"Good heavens! You really look pitiful in that dress. It could scare people away!" said the marquise.

Marion didn't flinch. As though hypnotized, she turned the little gold key in the lock on the box and lifted the lid.

## 6

Thirty-two flasks lined up in four rows filled three-quarters of the box. The remaining space contained perfume-making accessories. Marion dabbed the phials' glass stoppers with the tips of her fingers.

"Essences! Thank you, madame," she murmured, with so much emotion in her voice that Athénaïs seemed touched.

Marion lifted the flasks one by one to look at their labels. "Lavender . . . rosemary . . . rose . . . orange blossom, my favorite scent!" she said, smiling.

But her smile vanished when she saw the stunned look on the marquise's face.

"You know how to read! Who taught you?"

"I also know how to write," Marion replied, a touch of pride in her voice. She had turned away from the flasks and was fondling her medallion. "My mother taught me everything I know. My father thought I was too young, but she always disagreed. You'd think she knew what was in store for her."

"Your father carefully avoided mentioning this as part of your skills!"

Athénaïs looked furious, and Marion knew why. The nobility did not like commoners to know more than they did.

The marquise walked back to the little cabinet and returned carrying a second box, as well as a bottle of spirits.

"I hope that in the area of perfume, you'll be up to the task," she said. "I'd like you to create a fragrance that will be suitable for me in the heat of summer. These boxes contain all kinds of essences, and here's some alcohol," she said, setting the bottle down next to the boxes. "Now get to work!"

In a flutter of white silk, Athénaïs made an abrupt turn and noticed Pyrrhos sitting up on his hind legs and begging in front of the roast chicken. She pulled off a chicken wing and threw it up in the air. The spaniel swooped up and caught it; then he took it over to a bedside rug to gobble it in comfort.

Marion worked all night, oblivious to the hours going by. She almost forgot to replace the candles. The first box contained plant essences, which were lighter than the heady, spicy animal scents that were in the second box. She had started by opening every flask, one after the other, to smell their contents. Some fragrances were unknown to her. But now that she had smelled them, she would remember them forever. She would be able to recognize each one, even in small amounts, in any blend.

The sun was just rising as Marion placed a pretty crystal flask filled with a shimmering golden liquid on the console. She was happy. The perfume was ready. It was a unique, delightful fragrance, recalling a delicate, refined, blossoming bouquet.

"Madame la Marquise will be pleased," she said softly.

At that moment, she suddenly felt famished. She ate a bit of the pie and a chicken leg, then drank half the pitcher of orgeat milk.

She let herself settle comfortably in a blue silk armchair, nibbling at some fruit jelly while she waited for the favorite to wake up.

Outside, activity was slowly starting again. The château was waking up. Soon the footsteps of the marquise's women could be heard outside the door. Springing up, Marion returned to the stool and started untangling the skeins again.

Lucie was the first to enter the room. She sneaked over to her friend and hugged her.

"You didn't sleep! I knew it! Des Œillets will be surprised!"

The lady-in-waiting came in and drew open the bed curtains. After noting that the night had been peaceful, she announced that the tailor had just arrived. The marquise was in an excellent mood. She called Marion, who immediately handed her the flask. Athénaïs dabbed a drop of perfume delicately on the hollow of her wrist and smelled it.

"I like it. This is a fragrance that will go perfectly with the days of celebration to which the king is treating us." Then, addressing Claude des Œillets, she added, "From now on this girl will be one of my busy girls. Take her to the linen maids; she should be given clothes that are worthy of my household."

~ooo~

Marion thanked the marquise and left the bedroom. The side glances and whispers of the other servants as she went by didn't escape her notice.

On her way to the linen room, she felt a genuine tenderness for the marquise, whose blue eyes, she was certain, were windows opening onto an ocean of gentleness and kindness.

Indeed, hadn't the marquise tried to protect her by taking her in her arms on the day of the storm? Hadn't she allowed Marion to rest for several days after being injured? And by including her when she announced the great news of the king's return to Versailles, wasn't she letting Marion participate in the life of the court—she, the humblest of servants? Finally, thanks to the boxes, wasn't the marquise giving her the opportunity to indulge her passion for perfumes?

This woman was so kind that Marion felt completely overwhelmed. She was ready to serve her mistress with the utmost devotion. As far as she was concerned, Athénaïs de Montespan did not just have an angelic face. She *was* an angel.

Had Augustine Lebon and her father, who were responsible for her being in the favorite's service, been there at that moment, they would certainly have told Marion that angels may exist in heaven . . . but not on earth.

## 7

ℕews of the king's return had turned the favorite's quarters, particularly the linen room, into a beehive. Nearly all the servants here were buzzing about.

Marion would have gone unnoticed in the midst of all this bustle if, on entering this large room with white walls, Claude des Œillets had not shouted, "Mathilde, give this new girl a uniform. The marquise has chosen her to be one of her busy girls."

A fat, red-faced woman of about sixty, with gray hair and an unfriendly appearance, walked away from the table where she was folding sheets and waddled over to a small closet. Inside, in a jumble, were brick-colored linen dresses, fine nightgowns, aprons, slips, cotton stockings, bouffant bonnets with small embroideries, and shoes.

Marion stared in disbelief. The dress Mathilde had just placed on a chair was now hers. It was a simple servant's dress, the same as Lucie and the others wore, but she found it beautiful. It was her first real dress.

"The marquise chooses her busy girls in the crib

these days!" Mathilde said scornfully. "Try this on, you infant. It's the smallest one I have."

Marion looked around anxiously. "Here? In front of everyone?" she asked.

"Why not? They won't go blind from it, particularly since it looks to me as if you don't have much to show."

The linen maid laughed coarsely, offering her toothless mouth for all to see.

Reluctantly, Marion undressed. Wearing only her shabby underwear, she reached for the uniform but Fiacrine, another linen maid, grabbed the dress first and went up to Mathilde.

"She ain't very appetizing, the new girl, with her patched-up rags," Fiacrine said mockingly. "We'll have to tell the marquise she should think of buying underwear for her busy girls. This infant's underpants have so many stitches, she must be wearing her eyes out mending them. What a terrible shame! Her eyes are her best features! As for the rest, her mother didn't spoil her much! Look how skinny she is! I'll bet anything she hasn't had her first monthlies yet."

"Hand me that dress!" yelled Marion indignantly. "You and Mathilde are incredible vipers!"

A roar of laughter filled the room. Marion felt herself smarting with anger and wanting desperately to cry. Clenching her teeth and shutting her eyes, she tried as hard as she could to overcome her feelings. She didn't want any of these women to see her shed a single tear.

When she opened her eyes, they were dry, but her

heart was beating fast, pounding in her head, and everyone was staring at her.

Before she could reach for her dress, her head began to spin. She felt completely nauseated. The odor she hated most seemed to fill her mouth. Mixed with it were the smells of starch, burnt wood, dirt, and sweat that infested the air of the linen room. She then noticed that blood was trickling down from her nostrils.

"Zounds!" exclaimed Mathilde, slapping a wrinkled handkerchief onto Marion's face. "Looks as if her monthlies are coming out of her nose!"

"Let go of me, witch!" yelled Marion, struggling to free herself.

Just then Lucie came into the room and elbowed her way through the curious bystanders and the piles of linen. "You took advantage of Marion while I was busy with the marquise's toilette!" she shouted at everyone. "You, Mathilde, you're nothing but a shrew! You promised me you'd leave Marion alone! And all the rest of you here, staring! Don't you think Marion's been through enough being bitten by that nasty spaniel!"

"Hey! Calm down, my pretty," replied the old linen maid. "Can't we have a little fun? It's not my fault she's got a nosebleed. Or if it is, it would be the first time I made blood flow, not counting wringing the neck of a chicken! She's not strong and healthy, that's all!"

Mathilde and Fiacrine shrugged and set about their tasks again. In a wink they were engrossed in their work as though nothing had happened.

Marion was livid. She could not get rid of the blasted smell of blood. Lucie helped her dress and led her out of the linen room.

On the landing of the service stairs, they passed a tall woman dressed in black.

"There's the witch," Lucie whispered. "I've nicknamed her the Specter. The tailor has only just been admitted. She'll have to wait quite a while. Tough luck for her!"

Marion turned to see the Specter make her way toward Athénaïs de Montespan's small drawing room; then she handed her old clothes to her friend.

"Can you drop these off on my bed, please? I've got to go."

Turning on her heels, Marion tore down the stairs to the door of the courtyard. Lucie rushed to the banister and leaned down into the empty space, trying to catch sight of her friend.

"Marion, wait for me! Where are you going?"

## ❦ 8 ❦

Mechanically, with the tip of his knife, Antoine traced a cross on the bottom of a large loaf of fresh bread. He was starting to cut some thick slices when Gaspard Lebon ran into the kitchen.

"Your little girl is here!" Gaspard announced. "Augustine, add a plate!"

Antoine sprang to the doorway just in time to catch Marion in his arms. He held her very tightly and whirled her around, kissing her. Then, smiling, he put her down on the ground and stepped back to get a good look at her.

"Your dress is pretty and looks very good on you. But you're so pale!" Antoine said, suddenly alarmed. "You're not sick, are you? No one came for your belongings! No news for six days! We were all worried—weren't we, Augustine?"

"Antoine, stop assaulting her with questions," said Augustine. "Come here and give me a kiss, Marion. It's true, your dress is lovely, with that little décolletage setting off your medallion of the Virgin Mary. Be careful not to lose it! You'll have a bite to eat with us, won't you? By the way, does your employer feed you well? Tell us, we're eager to know what it's like at Montespan's."

"Put your mind at rest," replied Marion. "Her table is so lavish that three-quarters of the food goes back to the kitchen. Enough to feed her entire household!"

She went to snuggle up to her father and recounted everything that had happened in the last six days. Everything except the recent humiliating episode.

Antoine knitted his brows when he heard her tell about the storm and the dog. He and Augustine checked to make sure her wound had healed. Then everyone sat around the large table and ate heartily.

When they had finished their meal, they all returned to work. Before joining her father at the orangery, Marion took a walk around her dear orange trees, some of which were in bloom. The shiny leaves, the bark, the soil, even the wooden boxes in which the trees were planted, all these things gave off marvelous fragrances, which she alone could fully appreciate. Marion was happy to be back home. Here she breathed the gentle perfume of her childhood. While her father stood at the top of a stepladder trimming some branches, Marion discreetly entered the great gallery of the orangery. It was empty. Since it was summer, all the orange trees had been moved outside. All except the *Connétable*, because it required special care. This very old tree, with its gnarled trunk and large, dark leaves, was a legacy from François I. What a contrast with the pruned saplings!

Marion paused in front of them momentarily. The young trees were globe-shaped, like the older ones, but they were under twenty-five inches in height. These miniature orange trees were the king's latest gardening whim, and her father had created them.

As she whirled around enjoying the fullness of her skirt, Marion reached a small shed that was cold and humid inside and smelled of mildew. This was where the gardeners hoarded boards, flowerpots, tools, and old clothes. Marion knew she could also find empty bottles here. She picked one up, a small one, and slipped it into the pocket of her apron. With a look of determination, she made her way to the office of Monsieur Le Nôtre, the head gardener.

Le Nôtre was a man of genius, respected by everyone and loved by the king. He came to the shed almost on the sly, when he needed to work in peace and quiet. Here, surrounded by his beloved trees, he would design elaborate gardens and fountains.

Along the walls, a large number of little terra-cotta flowerpots were lined up on shelves. They contained cuttings and seedlings of various plants that were the subject of study. On the large worktable, rolls of paper were waiting for the master's appraisal, surrounded by all kinds of paraphernalia, such as pens, charcoal crayons, lead pencils, and bottles of ink.

Marion found a sheet of paper and a stool and sat down at the corner of the table to write. She would never dare to use Monsieur Le Nôtre's armchair! On the other hand, she had no qualms about borrowing one of his pens and his ink. She began writing her letters very industriously.

Succinctly, she confided on paper her joy in having created a perfume for the favorite and the suffering she had endured in acquiring her new dress. The cruelty of the linen maids was beyond her understanding. So was the indifference of the others, for no one had come to her defense except Lucie. With tears in her eyes, Marion raised her head and reflected for a moment. Who did these girls think they were? Was it possible that they had all forgotten their origins and, in the case of most, their past poverty?

Marion carefully rolled up the little sheet of paper and slipped it into the bottle.

On her way out of the orangery, she plucked a budding orange blossom and went to say goodbye to Augustine and Gaspard. She also took her belongings. With a tinge of sadness in his eyes, Antoine hugged her warmly and watched her walk in the direction of the gardens. He wondered when he would be seeing her again.

Marion followed the lanes down to a secluded area in the gardens, far from the paths where the courtiers strutted about in their fancy clothes trimmed with ribbons. She missed nature so much now that she was working for the marquise! When she was at the palace, she kept silent and tried not to be affected by the dreadful odors that assaulted her. That morning, she had found them unbearable. Had it been the smell of blood? The smell of the linen room, particularly nauseating and detestable because of the emotions associated with it? The smell of death clinging to the skin of the woman in black she had seen on the landing? The smell of the refuse littering the courtyard when she had run through it, pursued by the footmen's laughter?

She shut her eyes and took deep breaths, inhaling the light, perfumed air of the undergrowth. Then she took the little bottle out of her apron, slipped the orange blossom inside, and replaced the stopper. Ever since her mother's death, Marion, who spoke very little, had gotten into the habit of confiding all her secrets to the tall trees in the royal gardens. All she needed was a bottle, a few words jotted on a small sheet of paper, and an orange blossom, dried or freshly plucked. This last addition was an offering of sorts, a way of giving the trees that took her messages the sweetest perfume, the one she liked best of all.

Her eye fell on a great oak. She pulled up three handfuls of grass under it and dug into the earth with her hands. The soil was dry and light and sifted through her fingers. It smelled good.

She buried the bottle in the ground and stood up with a sigh. She felt relieved, as though she had just been delivered from a burden that was too heavy for her frail shoulders.

She leaned against the trunk and looked up at the sky sparkling between the foliage; then she let herself slip down to the ground.

Soothed by the scent of the grass, the moss, and the heather, her head resting on her bundle of belongings, Marion fell asleep. She knew the sap would carry her words from the roots of the oak all the way up to the top of the tree. The tall trees, their leaves rustling in the breeze, would whisper her secrets from branch to branch and leaf to leaf. . . . Her torments, joys, and dreams, confided to the earth of Versailles, would be swept up into the sky by the trees, just as a lost sailor puts all his suffering and hopes in a bottle he casts into the sea.

## ∽❧ 10 ❧∽

When Marion woke up, it was late afternoon. Attracted by some distant music, she walked over to the grand canal. All the vessels in the royal flotilla were on display before the king. Marion knew them well; her father had described them to her many times. Vividly colored cutters, brigantines, and feluccas vied with each other for the king's attention. Their reflections on the water played with the gold and orange rays of the late-afternoon sun. There were even two galiots with real galley slaves on board, and a miniature warship complete with cannons, carvings, riggings, and the flag bearing the king's arms. The sails flapped in the wind, and Marion could hear the cries of the sailors, with their Italian and Provençal accents.

The jewels of the flotilla were two golden gondolas, gleaming like brand-new coins. These two marvels had been given to Louis XIV by the ambassador of the Serenissima Republic of Venice, in the name of the doge, and had been brought to Versailles at considerable expense.

The king was aboard one of them. He wore a hat with

a magnificent plume and a suit studded with pearls and precious stones that sparkled in the warm sunlight. Athénaïs sat by his side, resplendent, and waved her fan with infinite grace. Her jewels glittered against the magnificent dress she had chosen for the king's return. A radiant smile lit up her face. She looked like a goddess.

The queen, short and stout, wore excessive makeup and was covered with gems from head to toe. She looked much less cheerful. Along with some noble ladies and a pack of tiny dogs, she was seated in the second gondola with the dauphin, the eldest son and only surviving child of the king and queen.

The king's musicians sailed behind the royal crafts in a cutter, playing the music of the well-known composer, Monsieur Lully. On the banks, courtiers, servants, and a motley crowd of curiosity seekers interpreted the sovereigns' every gesture and made comments. Marion also stood for a long time gazing at the king and the marquise, who were like two diamonds in a solid gold case.

Having grown up on the château grounds, Marion had always admired the sumptuous spectacle of Louis XIV's court. It was no wonder he was known as the Sun King. However, it seemed to her that she had never seen anything as beautiful as what she was seeing today. Her thoughts began to wander. . . . She recalled the January morning at the beginning of the year when the gondolas had glided on the icy water of the grand canal for the first time. The king, the whole court, and a huge crowd attended the event. Filled with wonder, Marion had promised herself that one day a handsome knight, a prince charming—a king, perhaps—would invite her to sit by his side in the gondola of her dreams. However, for a commoner, a poor servant, to imagine such a thing was extravagant, insane, pure madness!

Marion had never spoken about her fantasy to anyone—except, of course, to the earth of Versailles, her confidante for the last four years. Her rank certainly forbade such a dream from ever coming true, but she secretly believed in her future. Instinctively, she felt that in order to overcome fate, you had to entertain mad dreams. . . .

Marion's thoughts were interrupted when she saw Lucie and Martin Taillepierre coming toward her, hand in hand.

"There you are! Where were you?" asked Lucie.

"At the orangery. I wanted to see my father."

"The marquise heard about the nasty pranks the linen maids played on you. She sent people looking for you before going out for a stroll with the king. You know, he came to see her as soon as he arrived at the château!"

"Even before greeting the queen?"

"Yes, my girl! Everyone says that the festivities starting in four days are being given in her honor. The conquest of Franche-Compté is a mere pretext. She'll be the real queen of the fête!"

"Look!" cried Martin. "The gondolas are returning to the embankment. Let's go! We'll see the king close up!"

At thirty-six, the king was considered by many women to be the handsomest man in the kingdom. Marion and

Lucie heartily agreed. They watched as the king gracefully disembarked from the gondola and helped Athénaïs, who was carrying Pyrrhos under one arm, step ashore. Like all lovers, they had eyes only for each other and continued talking intimately.

Ignoring the crowd around them, they walked toward the tables that had been laid out under the trees for tea.

Martin, who knew how to elbow his way through a crowd, had positioned himself within earshot of them. When he rejoined Marion and Lucie, they bombarded him with questions.

"They didn't say anything unusual," he told them. "No, I assure you, they didn't say anything that might interest you."

"Stop teasing us!" Marion said.

"He just wants to keep us in suspense!" said Lucie. "Don't think I didn't notice the king's sly little smile. Come on, Martin, tell us what you heard!"

"Well, the king promised to join the marquise in the bath quarters this evening at ten o'clock, and to dine in her company. He also congratulated her on the perfume she was wearing, which was new to him. She told him it came from the workshop of a Florentine artisan in Paris who was very talented but whose prices are exorbitant. His Majesty immediately promised a substantial sum of money so long as her perfumer continued to provide excellent service."

"The king is even more generous than we think," said Lucie.

"Rather the lady is very clever," said Martin. "I'm willing to bet she'll gamble away all the money in one night and her Florentine will never see an ounce of gold." He shook his head. "Enough chatter! Sparks must be flying in the kitchen! I have to get back. Come see me at the rotisserie after dinner. I'll be able to give you a treat again!"

Martin ran off, and Lucie turned toward Marion.

"What do you think of that?"

"A perfumer in Paris," Marion answered in a flat voice. "Lucie, what perfume was the marquise wearing today? You were at her toilette this morning."

"I don't know. She puts on her perfume after the hairdresser does her hair. I had already left."

Marion shared her suspicions with Lucie; then the two friends followed the crowd and walked over to the buffet where the refreshments were spread out.

## 11

Six large tables were set up in a hexagon. They were covered with big white tablecloths, trimmed with fine lace, that reached down to the ground. Between each table was a globe-shaped orange tree. At the foot of the trees were baskets filled with flowers; they completely concealed the porcelain vases in which the trees were planted. Garlands of flowers, leaves, and ribbons, artfully intertwined, were strung up to the top of each tree. The orange trees were laden with all sorts of seasonal fruits, as though a miraculously varied harvest had sprung on one tree. The guests could help themselves.

Marion saw the king walk away from Athénaïs, who was devouring the cups of sherbet with her eyes. He went to the edge of the water to help the queen disembark from her gondola. She gave a stiff half-smile that showed how vexed she was at being neglected. She was also trying to hide her ugly teeth.

Knowing his wife's weakness for sweets, Louis led her directly to the table where a marzipan castle stood studded with caramels and candied fruit. All around it were tall crystal bottles filled with liqueurs and syrups. A little farther down were mountains of macaroons, almond cake with black currants, cream puffs, and all kinds of cookies. On another table, pyramids of figs, strawberries, and cherries were elegantly laid out between bowls of jam and fragrant compotes.

The queen's eyes shone.

Marion looked at the table where there were roasts decorated with feathers fanned out like peacock tails, perfectly baked pâtés, and luscious-smelling pies. She suspected Pyrrhos was not very far away! However, she saw only the marquise, billing and cooing, with a tight circle of people around her. Athénaïs laughed toothily, throwing her head back and flipping her fan open and closed. The king stood before her, enthralled.

Suddenly, a valet who was carrying a stack of dirty dishes heaped with leftover food stumbled and fell at Lucie's feet. The dishes made a dreadful racket as they fell to the ground and shattered. Marion sprang back to avoid being spattered with sauce. The waiter cursed when, in the middle of the debris, he saw the two plump quails that he had hidden under the leftovers for his own dinner. He no sooner stood up and adjusted his livery than Pyrrhos appeared on the scene. Marion had expected as much. In a flash, the spaniel snapped up one of the quails in his jaws and squatted on top of the other. He started to growl so fiercely that the valet surrendered his feast without a fight. The two girls bent down to help the poor fellow pick up the pieces of broken porcelain. Then Marion cautiously stepped close to Pyrrhos, who was chewing on the carcass in his jaw. The dog exuded a fragrance that Marion instantly recognized. It wasn't the creation of a Florentine perfumer—it was the very perfume she herself had created the night before.

## 12

"How beautiful!" marveled Marion as she walked around the spacious rooms in the bath quarters.

"Here everything is marble, precious fabric, gold, and silver. That was how the marquise wanted it, and the king had it all done according to her wishes," whispered Lucie. "Follow me, I'll show you the servants' rooms. Tonight you're in charge of the bouquets—the marquise's orders! She wants you to check on the harmony of the fragrances. Huge bunches of flowers have just been delivered to the pantry. Hurry! We have much to do before the king arrives!"

Marion and Lucie were in the hall preparing baskets of lilies, roses, and jasmine under the expert eye of Claude des Œillets when suddenly the apartment door was flung open. The favorite, glittering with jewelry, rushed in in a fury. She threw her gambling purse and gloves at the head of the Apollo statue, then charged across the drawing room. Her high heels rang out against the marble floor, and her golden locks bounced around her head like wild springs. Marion could hear a strange vibrato in the intonation of the marquise's voice that betrayed her rage.

"The king will not be coming!" Athénaïs shouted. "He changed his mind and will be dining in private at his wife's!"

"Is the queen unwell?" asked des Œillets, struggling to keep up with the favorite as she ran through the row of interconnected drawing rooms.

"No! His Majesty is angry, that's all! I lost six million at basset. That stupid game! I won four back almost immediately, but the king is mad at me anyhow! All because he'll have to take two million out of his own purse! What's two million for the king of France? A pittance!"

Marion was stunned. Even in several lifetimes her poor father couldn't earn what the marquise had just called a pittance.

Fuming, Athénaïs walked into the corner room, where the table had been set for supper. With the back of her hand, she knocked down a magnificent pyramid of fruits, which rolled onto the floor. Pyrrhos scurried around in all directions, not knowing what to bite into first.

With her confidante still hot on her heels, the favorite walked into the bath chamber, which was connected to the corner drawing room. She threw herself onto the large daybed and broke down in tears. The spaniel jumped up on the quilt and dropped an orange triumphantly at his mistress's feet. The marquise stopped crying.

An orange . . . That fruit was like a revelation to her. She instantly pulled herself together and regained her angelic demeanor.

"That's enough! I'm a Mortemart by birth! One of the greatest families in France! A Mortemart must not fall apart over such trivial matters. The queen is ugly, and her conversation is dreadfully boring. The king will come back to me! Within two days, at most, the Sun will be at my feet again!" She sighed, then turned to the table. "Oh! These emotions have made me hungry. Let's eat!"

With these words, Marion, Lucie, and all the others set to work again. Soon the marquise was served like a queen. The supper was sumptuous. Marion, who was helping by the plate warmer, delighted in the aromas of the various dishes that filed past her nose. These included orange-flavored lark pâtés, a rooster-comb pie with morels, pickled carp with crayfish bisque, a huge pike seasoned with saffron, and a veal ragout that had a nice fennel aroma. Then followed roasted pheasants and figs, a capon stuffed with lard and truffles, a large ham pricked with cloves, and a big piece of lamb seasoned with thyme. After that, lighter dishes were brought in— fricasséed asparagus and artichoke, baby peas with mixed herbs, and salads sprinkled with violets. A superb pyramid of fruits was reconstructed and served along with almond cream pastries, slices of fried melon, raspberry macaroons, and waffles with rose jam. Athénaïs then savored some fritters oozing with honey; she was like a sweet-toothed sultana in a harem. Marion watched her surreptitiously and understood that the marquise was trying to drown her frustration, not in tears, but in an excess of food, champagne, and strong liqueurs.

Finally, she satisfied her voracious appetite with peaches soaked in brandy and caramelized cherries with lime zest.

Soon after, her complexion turned gray, then yellow. She demanded a basin and a commode. The servants and valets looked at each other, dumbfounded. Was the marquise unwell?

Three of them ran to the wardrobe to get the commode and placed it in the bath chamber. Athénaïs staggered over to it, supported by two chambermaids.

Beauty triumphant, the queen of hearts of the greatest king in the world, was writhing with pain on her commode. A storm was brewing deep inside her noble entrails. Her birdlike stomach was letting loose, a debacle equaled only by the uncontrolled streams of vomit that nearly choked her. Marion thought there was justice after all. The beautiful Athénaïs was certainly being punished for her excesses . . . and for her lies, as well.

The foul-smelling odor wafting through the bath chamber was unbearable, especially for Marion.

Seeing that the marquise was in an extremely weak state, Claude des Œillets decided to summon Monsieur d'Aquin, the king's physician. Marion seized the opportunity to escape from the nauseating scene by volunteering to fetch him.

All evening, one thought had obsessed her: yes, she was still grateful to Madame de Montespan, but in the last few hours her trust had been mixed with vexation. It was beyond her understanding why the favorite had misled the king about her perfume. Aside from the money to pay off her gambling debts, what was she hoping to gain from this lie?

## ❦ 13 ❦

It was one o'clock in the morning. The lower gallery of the château was poorly lit and frightening. Marion made her way in the darkness, cupping the flickering flame of her candle. Where would this passageway lead? Lucie had explained how to get to d'Aquin's, but in the dark it wasn't easy.

Suddenly there was a rustling of cloth. Marion started. At first she saw nothing. Then she noticed a pair of lovers hidden in the shadow of a pillar. With the small halo of light from her candle, she quickly moved on, crossing through several corridors. She could hear the clopping of horses on the pavement outside, the screeching of coach wheels on gravel, and the laughter of people returning from a theater in Paris. She came across some stray dogs with their hind legs lifted, relieving themselves against the marble colonnades. And two men were lying on the ground at the foot of a stairway, dead drunk, wigs in hand, snoring loudly. They stank of tobacco, filth, and bad wine.

Marion felt sick. And here she had thought she would be sparing her nose by leaving the marquise's chamber!

Monsieur d'Aquin lived on the second floor. The narrow corridor that led to his apartment was full of smoke, and the smell of burnt fat added to Marion's nausea.

"Third door on the left," Lucie had said. Marion knocked on the door. In a flash, the physician's face appeared in the half-open door.

"What is it you want?" he asked in a husky voice.

Marion stood at the doorstep, speechless. The horrid odor of blood assaulted her. Dried blood that smelled of dust and death.

She swallowed. "I've been sent by Mademoiselle des Œillets. The Marquise de Montespan is ill. She has indigestion from overeating and—"

"And? What entitles you to give an opinion? Are you a physician? Sit down here and wait."

Marion entered the room, which was lit only with two candles, and watched d'Aquin collect his things.

"I'm no sooner back than I have to go out again!" the physician grumbled. "They'll kill me in the end, with their vapors and indigestion!" He looked at Marion. "Well, at least the sufferings of the good man I just left are over, God rest his soul!"

❧❧❧

Five minutes later, Marion and the physician were at the marquise's bedside. Her complexion was waxy and she seemed unconscious. Her ladies had placed her on the large daybed in the bath chamber, in the light of dozens of burning candles. The commode was still standing in the space between the bed and the wall, giving off its stench. It had not been emptied. Its contents were to be studied by the man of science to help him establish his diagnosis. In desperation, the servants had scattered sachets throughout the room and had burned perfumed pastilles. Marion was dying to open the widows wide to get rid of the putrid atmosphere and let in the fresh night air. But the shutters had been carefully drawn, for the marquise would never have tolerated a glimpse of the nocturnal sky. Marion wanted to throw up, for it seemed the odor of blood had trailed her. When she lowered her eyes, she discovered with horror that d'Aquin's shoes had traces of dried blood on them. Therefore, the smell was not tied to the physician's lodgings but to his person, and probably came from the patient he had spoken of earlier.

The man spread out his instruments and flasks of potions on a small table that had been covered with a white tablecloth and placed next to the bed. He casually raised the cover of the commode and leaned forward as though he were about to plunge his head inside.

"Quite extraordinary stomach fluid, and remarkably foul-smelling," he said with a solemn air as he straightened up.

At that moment, the marquise opened her eyes and requested a drink. The physician took her pulse.

"When you accompanied the king on his afternoon

walk, madame, it seems you were exposed to strong sunlight for too long," d'Aquin asserted. "As you know, the rays of the sun have a harmful effect on every part of the body. They heat up the bile, which flows suddenly into the stomach and bowels, causing perturbations in the liver. As for the dry mouth from which you are suffering, it is certainly due to that overflow of bile; it prickles the membranes of the esophagus and fills the mouth with a warm, dry vapor." He let go of the marquise's wrist. "You need a large glass of cool water, madame; it will dilute the bile and temper the heat in your internal organs. However, we must also administer a bleeding. This is unavoidable. We will administer it in the foot so as to draw the humors to the lower body and relieve your stomach. After that, an enema of rose water and honey will do marvels. Tomorrow you should take a bath."

Marion listened to this monologue and stood by during the medical procedures. Though tormented by nausea, she stayed put and took in every detail of the sickening sight.

The physician left one hour after his arrival, leaving the marquise inert and deathly pale. Marion handed him a candlestick at the small door that opened onto the lower gallery.

"Your mistress will probably have a restless night and bad dreams," said the physician. "That's quite an indigestion she's suffering from!"

"If that's the case, sir, why didn't you tell her so?"

Marion said. "She might show more self-control the next time around."

The physician shook his head. "Don't you know that the powerful of this world are irreproachable? They must never be held accountable, not even for their self-inflicted mishaps. So we physicians talk about the heat and the cold, humidity in the air, long horseback rides, the planets, and so on. What can you do? The king likes beautiful, plump, blond women who are as piggish as he is! One day, their gluttony will kill them all, you'll see! It's time to go to sleep now. I'm due at His Majesty's *lever* tomorrow at seven; that's when he rises. Farewell!"

## ∾ 14 ∽

By the time Marion returned to the bedroom in the bath quarters, Lucie alone was attending to Athénaïs.

"The marquise has recovered enough strength to give out orders," she told Marion. "She wants you to watch over her again tonight. She also wants you to create another perfume. But this one is for a man—the duke de Vivonne, her brother; she wants to make him a gift. Here are the boxes of essences she asked me to fetch. Do you want me to stay with you?"

"No, Lucie. I'm not sleepy, everything will be fine. Go to bed. You look exhausted."

As soon as her friend had left, Marion checked all the candles, shook the sachets, and placed new pastilles in the incense burners. Athénaïs was sleeping peacefully, so Marion seized the moment and sat down in an armchair to think. In this palace, barring a few exceptions, stench was sovereign, and she desperately wanted to find a way of sparing her nose. Wherever she went, whatever she did, odors assailed her, and one day she feared they would permanently ruin her sense of smell.

Marion knew that to protect themselves, surgeons covered their faces with long, beak-shaped masks filled with fragrant herbs. Obviously she could not wear such trappings in the marquise's service. But there had to be something equally effective yet invisible.

As her thoughts drifted, Marion looked around the room. Suddenly, her eyes settled on a magnificent bouquet she had arranged with Lucie's help. She sprang out of the armchair as an amusing idea came to her. Masking bad smells with a large quantity of perfume wasn't a solution she favored, so she was determined to create an elixir that would absorb bad odors, making them disappear. If she could dab a drop of such a liquid on the edge of her nostrils, it would trap and obliterate foul odors and protect her sense of smell. This was a novel, extremely bold idea for a young girl who had only a rudimentary knowledge of perfume making and owned no equipment. No matter! She would try nonetheless.

Her idea was based on a simple principle. In order to fight stench, Marion had to use white flowers, known for their purity. She had to tightly wrap them in linen drenched in oil, for grease had the property of absorbing every hint of scent. Soon the withered petals would turn into a grayish, translucent mass, so odorless that even Marion couldn't detect a trace of their former fragrance. Then she would soak this mass of withered and odorless flowers in spirits and press it. The potion that she extracted would have a remarkable property: it would quickly absorb and trap every kind of odor, as a dry sponge retains drops of water.

Marion went through the rooms of the bath quarters collecting all the white flowers she could find in the vases.

Soon she had piled up a large quantity of beautiful, pearly, silky petals on a large sideboard table in the pantry. Jasmine, camellias, roses, lilies, tuberoses, iris, and orange blossom perfumed the air.

Marion searched the storeroom and found two big bottles of oil and a pile of white linen. She took a large porcelain basin, in which she placed the flowers wrapped in linen, then poured oil over the cloth until it was fully saturated; afterward, she placed a platter on top of the linen and weighted it to press the flowers. Now she had to wait. She hid the basin under a piece of furniture and returned to the marquise's bedside. She planned to visit Augustine Lebon in the morning to get the required amount of spirits.

~~~

As d'Aquin predicted, the marquise slept very fitfully. She slowly regained color in her cheeks, but her breathing was rapid and her restless head movements were a sign that she was having nightmares. Marion now had to obey orders and create a perfume. She drew a chair up to the table the physician had used and set to work. She was measuring out the essences and mixing them very carefully when suddenly the marquise let out a shrill cry. Marion almost dropped her flasks. Putting her work aside, she rushed to the bed.

The beautiful Athénaïs was red in the face and drenched in sweat. Pyrrhos was stretched flat at the foot of her bed, his head between his front paws, staring and rolling his eyes.

Marion wondered if she should summon d'Aquin again, but the marquise began speaking. Her voice was deep, unrecognizable, almost frightening, and her words were badly articulated.

"The queen is just a puppet used by the king of Spain to blackmail France. . . . 'Watch out; if Louis XIV doesn't marry my daughter, we'll wage war against you!' . . . The king yielded for reasons of State. . . . That silly, ugly Infanta! The marriage is a fraud. . . . I was the only match worthy of the king. . . . I'm a Mortemart, after all! My family's aristocratic ancestry is much older than the Bourbons'. . . . I was born to be queen, my astrologer told me so again this morning, and soon she will provide me with the means to ascend the throne. I shall be queen of France! Do you hear?"

Marion frowned. The marquise's delirium was alarming. How would the soothsayer provide Athénaïs with the means to become queen of France? What was the favorite alluding to? Was the queen in danger?

The marquise was now sitting up in bed, eyes wide open and arms outstretched. Seeing her extreme restlessness,

Marion thought that Athénaïs had finally woken up. But that was not the case. The favorite fell back on her pillows, still flushed and drenched, but calmer, and she soon fell sound asleep.

~⌒∽⌒∽~

Marion returned to her table in a pensive state and quickly finished her work. She had another preoccupation: who would get credit for her new perfume? She suspected it would be an artisan from Florence or elsewhere, some figment of the marquise's fertile imagination, for it was clear she had decided to keep Marion well in the background. This gave Marion a heavy heart.

But then, when she reflected on how quickly she had risen in the world, she regained her self-confidence. One day, she was sure, her work would be recognized and she would have a better future.

In the early hours of the morning, Marion opened the gilded shutters with their decorative carvings of dolphins. She held her Virgin medallion in her hand and allowed her thoughts to wander as she watched the mist rise over the flowerbeds. A bright new day full of promise was dawning on the horizon.

"**A** bath! Can you imagine, sire, that your chief physician, d'Aquin, wanted me to take a bath! I flatly refused," said Athénaïs. "It would certainly have wilted my stamina and my brain. I would have become as dumb as a dodo bird, while you can see how I am as fresh and lively as can be!"

Indeed, two days after her indigestion, the marquise had recovered and had moved back into her quarters. The king, who had paid and forgiven his beautiful lady's gambling debts, had promised to visit her that morning, after the council meeting.

Marion had noticed that when he announced he would be coming, Athénaïs had raised her pretty chin triumphantly.

❦❧

Marion was in the kitchen area when the king arrived at the marquise's. When she returned to the large drawing room with a tray full of pastries, she found them very quietly talking about the days of celebration that were soon to begin. Marion felt intimidated, for this was the first time she had been so close to Louis XIV. As for the king, he paid no more attention to her than to a speck of dust fluttering in a ray of light. He was sitting in a wide armchair, legs crossed. Pyrrhos lay in front of him, his nose resting on the point of the king's shoe, his chops curled up, his teeth bared. As always, he was growling.

The favorite had been living in the monarch's shadow for seven years and had grown to know him well. Today she thought he looked troubled. Was it because of affairs of State, or did he still hold a grudge against her? The king seemed to guess her thoughts.

"Madame, the Count de Peyrussel died two days ago, and I am most unhappy about it," he explained. Seeing Athénaïs's astonished look, he continued, "Truly a very sad piece of news! It happened while you yourself were unwell. I had great esteem for that elderly man. He had shown his devotion to the Crown on many occasions. It wasn't so long ago that no one thought anything of betraying the king. I never forgot those who remained loyal to me."

"Sire, is it known what he died of?" asked the marquise.

"From what I was told, the count arrived home at around ten, after the card games, his face contorted, a wild look in his eyes, and in such a state of excitement that it was initially believed he was having a fit of madness. He ran to his wife's bedroom and started to jump up and down on the bed. Then he leaped all around the room from one armchair to another before collapsing on the floor, foaming at the mouth and shaking convulsively." The king sighed. "The countess rushed to the queen's quarters, where I was dining, and begged me on her knees to send my physician. I consented immediately. D'Aquin administered three bleedings. But if you ask me, bleedings are not the universal remedy for all ills. Whatever the case, the count had regained his wits by the time the priest came to administer the last rites. Poor Peyrussel finally breathed his last in the midst of a confession that consisted of incoherent babbling."

Suddenly the king's voice hardened.

"This morning I read the report of the surgeons who performed the autopsy. They are unequivocal: the cause of death was poison!"

"Really?" cried the marquise indignantly. She raised to her lips a glass of liqueur Marion had just given her. "But who could have committed such a crime? And why?"

"I have no idea, madame. But I'll find out, believe me! Paris and its suburbs are swarming with alchemists, perfumers, and other soothsayers who are actually sorcerers and poisoners. They run prosperous businesses just as though they were honest shopkeepers. This will not last! I will have them arrested, cross-examined, and burned at the stake. I intend to purge the kingdom of this dangerous vermin! I'll do whatever it takes, in time and expense. And I swear before God that I'll succeed!"

At the mention of perfumers, Marion had shuddered nearly as much as the marquise had at the mention of soothsayers. The king noticed his favorite's discomfort.

"I see I'm tiring you, madame," he said, rising to his feet. "You must still be weak from the ailment that kept you in bed for two consecutive days. Would you give me the pleasure of joining me tomorrow at the Trianon for my stroll? You'll find the air there is invigorating, and Monsieur Le Nôtre assures me the flowerbeds are gorgeous. Might I add that, for me, your presence will make them even lovelier?"

Athénaïs bowed in one of the gracious curtseys that were her specialty. "Thank you, Your Majesty, I'll be there."

The king returned to his quarters, and the marquise announced that she wished to lunch alone in her bedroom.

As for Marion, she was already daydreaming about the thousands of flowers and bewitching perfumes in the gardens of the Trianon de Porcelaine. She hoped the favorite might allow her to go along.

## ～❧ 16 ❧～

**M**arion raced up the stairs leading to the attic and rushed into her room.

"I was waiting for you so we could go join Martin in the kitchens," said Lucie. "He promised to keep a pâté and some fritters for us."

"Wait, Lucie! I have something to show you."

Marion opened the door of a little closet set in the wall right next to her bed. She took out a glass flask full of a transparent liquid with mauve reflections.

"That perfume has a strange color!" said Lucie, surprised. "Did you make it?"

"It isn't a perfume, but a potion I created to capture the bad odors I can't abide anymore."

"How did you make that? It isn't witchcraft, is it?"

Marion explained how the idea had come to her and the methods she had used to carry it out.

Lucie gaped as she listened. "And does it work?"

"I don't know. I haven't tried it yet. But we'll soon know if it meets my expectations."

Marion undid the stopper and with her fingertip put a

drop of the pearly liquid under each of her nostrils. She handed the flask to her friend. Lucie imitated her, hesitating a bit. After carefully replacing the flask in the closet, they left the room.

The foul smell that usually floated through this level of the château would be an excellent test. The heat of early summer aggravated the stench of the meals being fried on the burners by some of the servants, as well as the poorly washed chamber pots, the pails filled with refuse, the dust, the mice droppings, and the dirty dishes soaking in basins.

The two friends made their way slowly down the long corridor, staring straight ahead. From time to time they turned their heads and sniffed, raising their noses slightly.

Nothing. They couldn't smell a thing! When they were absolutely convinced of this, they threw themselves into each other's arms and burst out laughing. The other servants, who noticed their behavior, wondered what game could possibly be so amusing.

Marion and Lucie held hands and hurtled down the stairs to get lunch. Along the way, they passed by the linen room, which was nearly deserted at that hour. Only Mathilde and Fiacrine were there, sitting in a corner eating soup. Not the slightest odor reached the girls' noses, and they immediately set off again, laughing even more merrily.

When they entered the rotisserie where Martin

worked, their joy was suddenly dampened. The potion had an effect that they hadn't anticipated: it canceled out the good smells that enchanted them whenever they walked into the kitchen.

The plump guinea fowls that glided past their noses before flying to the marquise's table had no aroma; they might as well have been papier-mâché!

The two friends looked at each other, surprised and frustrated.

"Don't worry!" said Martin, misinterpreting their dejected look completely. "I've kept something for us that I think you'll like!"

He took three plates out of a sideboard and placed them on the enormous table occupying the center of the kitchen.

Marion and Lucie brought tumblers, knives, and bread while Martin went to the storeroom.

He returned with a triumphant air, carrying a shiny, golden pâté; its crust was so beautifully decorated that it seemed a shame to cut into it.

"It's all fresh! I prepared it this morning," Martin said proudly. "The meat simmered in a bouillon of herbs and spices. Smell it!" He held the plate out in front of his friends, who pretended they could appreciate its aroma.

Marion had no idea how long the effect of her potion would last. She was afraid it might also deprive them of their sense of taste.

Fortunately, though the pâté had no aroma, it was absolutely delicious. The young cook was justly proud of his creation. It occurred to Marion that his gift for blending flavors was like her gift for blending fragrances.

Before Marion and Lucie left, Martin suggested they take along the rest of the pâté and some fritters, and he wrapped them in a dish towel. The girls thanked him.

As they went up to the attic, they passed Claude des Œillets on the first-floor landing. Marion realized the potion was beginning to wear off. She had just caught a whiff of the dreadful geranium-based perfume the attendant doused herself with every day.

Lucie, who noticed it as well, smiled and whispered into her friend's ear, "You're a magician."

The elixir's quasimagical effect had lasted for about half an hour.

"Marion, I told you several times that you should sleep this afternoon," said des Œillets, a trace of annoyance in her voice. "The marquise wants you to watch over her tonight and go with her to the Trianon tomorrow."

Marion was thrilled. Her potion was effective beyond all expectation, and tomorrow she would be included with the favorite in the king's stroll.

As for sleep, it was out of the question. Only one thing was important—confiding her happiness to paper and to the earth of Versailles. On her way to fetch a bottle and an orange blossom at the orangery, she would drop in on Augustine Lebon and tell her that tomorrow she would finally get to see the Trianon de Porcelaine. She could already hear the dear woman's amused response: "Heavens, the marquise really can't do without you anymore!"

The coach carrying the marquise's ladies had just driven through the gates of the Trianon de Porcelaine. Claude des Œillets had decided that Lucie and two other chambermaids would also be included on the trip.

Marion was amazed by what she saw—an enchanted palace in blue and white, sparkling in the warm sun of early July. The round courtyard was ringed by five pavilions. The little palace, made entirely of porcelain, was decorated like the marquise's china incense burners. Everything was blue and white: the gates and the window panels, the cherubs and the earthenware birds on the cornices of the roofs.

"The apartments are in the central pavilion, and the offices and service rooms in the four smaller buildings on each side of the courtyard," Lucie explained.

The king and his guests had not yet arrived. The servants and gardeners were rushing around attending to last-minute details.

"This trunk weighs a ton!" complained Lucie, for whom the magic of the place had long ceased to be moving.

Marion was pulled out of her reverie and rushed to her friend's aid.

"This happens every time!" said Lucie. "You'd think the marquise was coming to stay for three days when she's only been invited for the afternoon. True, this place is a bit like home to her. The king had it built in her honor." Lucie indicated all the buildings with a sweeping gesture of her head. "He'll do just about anything to please her!"

Marion, still very troubled by the favorite's ravings on the night she had suffered from indigestion, took advantage of this last comment.

"Do you think he would go so far as to propose marriage to her if the queen were to pass away?"

"That's a very odd question!" said Lucie. "Don't forget that the marquise is already married. For the king to marry her, she would have to be a widow. And last I heard, Monsieur de Montespan was in excellent health. As for the queen, she's also in excellent health. No, there's no wedding in sight, my lovely!"

"But isn't that what the marquise would like?" Marion pressed.

"Oh, yes! She's already fuming that she can't be a duchess!"

"And why can't she be?"

Lucie laughed. "Aren't you satisfied being the perfumer of a marquise?" she teased. "Or is it your dream to work for a queen or duchess?" She looked around to make sure no one besides Marion was within earshot;

then, becoming serious again, she added, "The marquise has begged the king several times to make her a duchess. But for that to happen, Monsieur de Montespan would have to be made a duke. His Majesty will never grant him that favor."

"How do you know that?"

"Because the king said so in my presence."

"In your presence! I don't believe it! Don't they wait until they're alone before discussing such delicate personal matters? I suspect you listened at the door!"

Lucie shook her head. "No need to listen at the door! Haven't you noticed they're always surrounded by servants? We're invisible as far as they're concerned. We're blind and deaf. We have no brains with which to think and no tongues with which to gossip. So they talk about everything in our presence. Why should they deny themselves?"

"You mean we're like furniture?"

"No, Marion. Their furniture is worth a fortune; we're worth nothing. All they notice is our work. As persons, we don't exist. You had better get used to this or you'll always be unhappy."

The two friends leaned down to grasp the handles of the trunk. They had difficulty lifting it. Marion felt sad. Lucie wasn't informing her of anything new, but she was outraged by such indifference. She knew that deep down she would never get used to it.

Once they had left their heavy load in the wardrobe of the central pavilion, Lucie drew Marion outside.

"Come with me. There's a spot here I know you'll like."

They walked toward the gardens and, like two little mice, slipped behind the trellis fences that ran along the flowerbeds. Monsieur Le Nôtre was right; they were magnificent.

Soon the girls arrived in front of a little house that was blue and white like the other buildings. The doors were wide open in anticipation of the king's arrival.

"This is the cabinet of perfumes, a true gold mine for you," Lucie said, smiling. "That is, providing you haven't dabbed your nostrils with the potion we tested yesterday!"

Marion laughed. "No, I haven't used it. But I've got the flask in my pocket. You never know!"

She looked around. The cabinet resembled a drawing room, luxuriously decorated with refined taste, but it was actually a kind of greenhouse bursting with fragrant plants.

"How marvelous!" exclaimed Marion. "All these flowers are rare pearls, gems, treasures! They could be used to make hundreds of fabulous perfumes."

Marion was fluttering like a butterfly from one plant to another when all of a sudden Lucie caught her by the arm and pulled her toward the exit.

"Come on, we've got to return to the Trianon. The guests are already there, and the king will be arriving soon with the queen and the favorite."

"If, as you say, the marquise is the mistress here, perhaps she'll give me permission to use these plants to make fragrances," said Marion.

"Don't count on it! This isn't a laboratory but a place of relaxation, where the king and the marquise come to rest during the summer heat waves."

Marion left the cabinet of perfumes with regret. She stopped in the doorway, momentarily pensive.

"I have a strange feeling that something will draw me back here, and that I'll be returning soon," she said.

## ~ 18 ~

**M**arion and Lucie left the cool shade of the pavilion and returned unnoticed to the small palace.

The king had already started on his stroll. The cortège stopped on the terraces to admire the orange trees, pomegranate trees, and jasmine bushes. Louis XIV was very fond of the Trianon gardens, where the harmonious colors competed in splendor with the fragrances.

Suddenly an unusual shudder ran through the assembled company. From the service rooms, Marion and Lucie saw that Queen Marie-Thérèse and several other ladies, including the marquise, were unwell. Lucie ran to the wardrobe, opened a trunk, and took out a flask of smelling salts. The two friends darted over to the group.

"There isn't a patch of shade or a breath of air," murmured Marion.

"And as usual, the ladies are suffocating in their tight corsets," added Lucie.

The heat in the gardens was crushing, and the

scent of the blossoming flowers was so intoxicating and heady, it was nauseating. The air had become oppressive.

Marion, who was beginning to feel faint herself, quickly dabbed a drop of her potion under each nostril. The effect was immediate. She realized that smelling salts would be useless in this circumstance. Only her elixir could be effective.

But then she recalled the marquise's betrayal concerning her perfume. She hesitated a moment. . . . Should she forget her grudge? Should she help the favorite and offer her potion? Or should she let her sniff the repellent, malodorous smelling salts?

Marion's generosity prevailed. She administered her potion, and Athénaïs sat up, looking radiant. She stared at Marion as though she were seeing her for the first time; then she exchanged a knowing glance with Claude des Œillets. Marion was worried by this exchange.

A few steps away, the poor queen sat on a bench surrounded by her ladies-in-waiting, dwarf jesters, and dogs. She sneezed over and over again and moaned in Spanish.

❧❧❧❧❧

Eventually the sovereign, too, grew weary of the burning sun and the overabundance of heavy fragrances. To his guests' great relief, he signaled that it was time to return to the Trianon. They all headed for the tables that had been set up in a shady thicket of trees for a light refreshment.

Exhausted, Marie-Thérèse preferred to take refuge inside. The king promised to join her soon. Athénaïs decided to accompany the queen, taking Claude des Œillets, Marion, and Lucie along with her. Pyrrhos trotted behind them, his tongue hanging out of his mouth, clearly dying of thirst.

The queen stretched out on a couch. Marion was astounded by the ambience of this room. How could one possibly live in such a stupendous décor?

Here again, the dominant color scheme was blue and white. The carved paneling of the bed, the floor, the walls, and all the other furniture blended into a kind of exotic delirium. There were mirrors, paintings, tapestries and drapery, ribbons and lace everywhere she looked.

The queen and the marquise talked about the approaching days of festivities. The favorite remarked that the king would miss the playwright Moliére, who had died eighteen months ago. Marie-Thérèse, who loved to eat, was looking forward to the marvelous supper that would be served after the entertainment. But neither of the two women spoke about what they planned to wear. Each one hoped to dazzle the king and outdo her rival. Athénaïs looked down on the queen with compassion. She was convinced she had already won the battle. Her thoughts were so clearly reflected in the expression on her face that the queen took offense. Cutting the conversation short, Marie-Thérèse clapped her chubby little hands and gave out orders in Spanish. She requested macaroons and chocolate. Marion and Lucie were told to transmit the orders to the kitchen.

～⌒∾⌒⌒∾～

After this was done, Marion decided to go and rest in the wardrobe of the central pavilion, where she had spotted a camp bed. She had had almost no sleep for two days. As she was about to leave the service rooms, she noticed that the potion's effects had worn off. Her attention was drawn by an unknown smell.

Intrigued, she went up to a draining board where a stack of dirty dishes lay. She could see the remains of a thick brown liquid at the bottom of a small receptacle that looked like the coffeepots she had seen at the marquise's. She recognized the smell of milk, sugar, cloves, and vanilla mixed together. But there was some other ingredient. She could tell from the color, but also from an aroma that dominated all the others.

"Haven't you seen a dirty chocolate pot before?" said a kitchen boy who was passing by. He laughed.

So, this appealing fragrance, sweet and intense, a delicate blend both bitter and mild, was the much-talked-about cocoa!

Marion put her index finger into the remaining drops of the drink and tasted it. It was delicious!

∽⌇∾

When Marion woke up about two hours later, the courtiers were gone. Everything was quiet. As she came out of the wardrobe to join Lucie, she saw the sovereign cross the hall with Monsieur Le Nôtre. They were engrossed in a conversation concerning the orange trees that would be required to set the scene for the festivities of July fourth. Marion curtsied, but the king didn't notice her.

When he walked by, she inhaled something that instantly brought tears to her eyes.

Where could Lucie be? She finally found her in the courtyard in front of the service rooms. Lucie had been looking for her, too. Seeing that something was troubling Marion, she drew her aside.

"Why do you look so upset?"

"I'm in despair, Lucie. The marquise has betrayed me again. Remember, the night she was sick, she wanted me to make a perfume for her brother? Well, I just walked by the king, and he's wearing it! I'd recognize that perfume anywhere, like all the ones I make myself. Why did she lie to me?"

"I have no idea."

"And to think I thought she had a heart of gold! Had I known, I would never have offered her my potion!" cried Marion. "I should have let her poison herself with the smelling salts!"

Lucie took her by the arm. "You must pull yourself together, dear. The marquise has decided to go to the Château de Clagny. We'll be leaving in a few minutes, and this time, we'll be traveling in the same coach as her. She must not see you in this state!"

## 19

Indeed, at about six o'clock in the evening, the marquise had suddenly decided to leave the Trianon and go to Clagny, where Louis XIV was having a new palace built for her. She wanted to see for herself how the construction was progressing.

The coach was tossed about as it raced down the bumpy road. Inside, they all hung on for dear life. Fortunately, the ordeal wouldn't last long; the Château de Clagny was near Versailles.

Marion scrutinized the favorite, who was sitting opposite her. Her face still looked angelic; her gestures were extremely graceful and her voice crystal clear. Yet Marion knew that she would never again see Athénaïs as when she had first seen her. This woman was unjust, she was a liar, and her reputation as a schemer was probably deserved. Marion felt tears welling up in her eyes again. How could she have been so wrong? She quickly pulled herself together, for now the marquise was staring back at her.

"Why are you looking at me in that way?" the marquise snapped. "Do I have a crooked nose?"

Athénaïs's bad mood was obvious.

No one spoke anymore until Clagny. Marion looked out the window of the coach, happily breathing the warm, fragrant country air.

Soon the coach slowed down and took a bend in the road. Marion saw the favorite's château looming on the horizon. *It's a second Versailles!* she thought.

Indeed, at Clagny, as at Versailles, there was scaffolding everywhere. Crowds of workers were bustling about in the midst of heaps of sand, rubble, tools, and stone blocks.

The coach made its way through the cluttered courtyard and dropped the marquise and her entourage off at the front steps. She led the way up to her quarters, with Pyrrhos at her heels.

The bedroom was heavily decorated with gilding, and a strong, unpleasant odor of paint hung in the air. Since the mistress's visit was unexpected, all the furniture was still covered with white sheets.

Claude des Œillets helped the marquise change into a simpler, lighter dress, and Marion and Lucie folded the gown embroidered with natural pearls that the favorite had worn at the Trianon. They were about to put it away in the trunk when they heard a carriage enter the courtyard. Putting down the dress, they went to a window. A tall woman dressed in black stepped out of the carriage and climbed the front steps. In spite of the mask and veil covering her face, she was perfectly recognizable.

"Well, well!" murmured Lucie. "It's the Specter. So the marquise's architectural concerns were an excuse. The truth is, she has an appointment with la Voisin, that accursed witch! Those two are so talkative, we'll be here for two hours! During that time I can show you the gardens. They're as beautiful as the ones at the Trianon!"

"Go without me, Lucie. I'm not in the mood. I'd rather stay in the pantry and rest in case the marquise wants me to watch over her tonight."

"If you like."

Marion made believe she was going to the service rooms, but as soon as Lucie was gone, she went back to the marquise's bedroom. It was deserted, but voices could be heard from an adjoining private chamber. Marion sneaked up to the door hidden behind drapes. She pressed her ear against it and recognized the marquise's voice. . . .

## 20

"A black mass! Again!" cried the marquise. "I fear the devil, madame! I am sick of lying naked on a pallet while you consecrate the host with the blood of a newborn child! Don't forget, I'm the mother of three princes whom the king has just made legitimate. From now on, my rank forbids me to engage in such eccentricities!"

"Your face will be masked, as it always has been, Madame la Marquise. No one will be able to recognize you, any more than before."

"It's become too risky! There are too many envious people at the court spying on me and seeking my downfall. I can get the king to do anything I want. My favor has never been more dazzling. I risk losing it all if I'm found out!"

"Remember, madame, the black masses, which you want to give up, are the reason for your good fortune, as are the powders you've had the king take for years."

"I know."

"May I also remind you that your dearest wish was to supplant the former favorite? The king was very attached to Mademoiselle de La Vallière for years. Yet you triumphed, and she's now cloistered in a Carmelite convent. Do you need any further proof of how effective our ceremonies and the potions I've made for you are?"

"Small victory!" cried the marquise. "The king sent La Vallière away, but he didn't repudiate the queen. You're trying to fool me with your tales of sorcery! I'm paying you a high enough price; you should follow my orders. Where is the quick and efficient method you mentioned to me?"

"Here it is," said la Voisin with a sigh. "It's a powder that has a radical effect. I made it from an Italian recipe."

"Excellent! As soon as I become queen, I'll make you the richest witch in the kingdom."

Marion was horrified. Her suspicions were now confirmed: Athénaïs de Montespan had not been raving incoherently in her sleep. She had simply betrayed her inner thoughts! She truly intended to get rid of the queen.

Bending down carefully, Marion peered through the keyhole. The two women were sitting facing each other, on opposite sides of a table. The sorceress had just placed a small copper tube in front of the marquise. Marion also saw Pyrrhos, who suddenly yelped as he looked at the door. The dog was aware of her presence, but the favorite was so absorbed in her conversation, she was not paying attention to him.

"I beg you, listen to me, Madame la Marquise. A black

83

mass is essential. If it can't be said over you in person, it can be said over the body of a woman you appoint to represent you."

The marquise frowned. "That means one more person would be in on the secret! I don't like the idea. Still, if it's vital, I'll find someone. See to it that the ceremony takes place tomorrow evening."

"The problem is, Madame la Marquise, a black mass requires a sacrifice," said la Voisin, leaning over the table. "I don't know if we'll be able to get a newborn baby by tomorrow."

"As I recall, an infant is worth no more than an ecu. I'm prepared to pay ten," shouted the favorite as she grabbed a piece of paper and a goose quill. "Now find me one!"

Athénaïs continued to speak while she was writing. "Tomorrow, I'll give this note summarizing all my wishes to the person I'll have chosen. That's how you'll know who she is. Since I won't be present, I'd like these words to be read during the ceremony."

Marion, stunned by the scene she had just witnessed, lost her balance and fell to the floor. Pyrrhos began barking immediately.

She had to hurry! She couldn't just hide. The spaniel would trace her scent. She took the flask out of her pocket and sprinkled a few drops of her potion on the ground, on the spot where she had fallen. Then she rushed to hide under a console covered by a white sheet.

Her mouth was dry, her throat was tight, and she was

trembling all over. The sound of her wild heartbeats echoed so loudly in her ears, she hardly heard the door of the chamber open. Fortunately, she could see what was going on through a tiny hole in the fabric.

As predicted, Pyrrhos began to sniff the ground, growling. The marquise and the sorceress watched him intently.

At first the spaniel seemed to have found Marion's trail, but then his nose came up against her potion. He shook his head, squatted, and wagged his tail, staring up at his mistress with a contented air.

"That dog is stupid," the marquise decided, shrugging. Then, turning to la Voisin, she handed the woman a well-stuffed purse and added, "Do you know that Pyrrhos was possessed by the demon during the last storm? He bit the girl I was clasping against me, as you had advised. She was a flimsy shield, but still, you were right. There's nothing like an innocent child to ward off the specter of death!"

Marion couldn't believe her ears. All along she had thought the marquise had wanted to protect her, or at least reassure her, during the storm. How wrong she had been!

The two women disappeared into the antechamber, and Marion heard their steps grow distant as they made their way down the formal stairway. Pyrrhos followed them, so the coast was clear.

Marion wanted to know more. Though her stomach was tied in knots from fear, she went into the chamber, read the note, and in a few seconds had learned it by heart. Then she opened the copper tube lying on the table and smelled its contents. They included dried blood and a mixture whose components even Marion couldn't distinguish. But one thing was certain: she would remember this dreadful odor.

## 21

"**C**an you imagine that the king had a ridiculous house built for me, one that could barely satisfy a mere dancer's whims! It wasn't to my taste, so he had it torn down and built Clagny instead."

In the coach returning to Versailles with her ladies, the marquise was visibly nervous; she spoke nonstop and giggled nervously. As always, she was in a hurry.

"Faster, coachman!" she shouted.

The coach was speeding down the road. The sun was setting, and Marion watched the rose-colored landscape roll by, glowing under the last rays of the sun.

Suddenly, the coachman started to curse. The horses neighed. The coach swerved and screeched to a halt in a cloud of dust. Claude des Œillets looked to see what had happened and cried out.

"What's going on?" asked the marquise, frowning.

People ran to the scene from all sides, raising their arms to the sky. Marion and Lucie exchanged looks full of dread.

Unfortunately, their fears were confirmed. As they stepped out of the coach, they saw a young man lying on the ground, his limbs at odd angles, his head thrust back, and his face bathed in blood. A woman was leaning over him, sobbing.

"My son! You've killed my son!" she yelled. "He was deaf; he couldn't hear your buggy coming down the road! You murderers!"

"The coach was racing full speed ahead," the coachman explained to Athénaïs. "There was nothing I could do! The horses collided with him, and the poor lad was thrown over to the side of the road. His head must have hit a large rock."

The marquise glanced out the door but didn't take the trouble to step down.

Marion went back inside the coach. Tears were streaming down her face. This was a ghastly accident! And the smell of blood was making her nauseated.

Propped up on her cushioned seat, the favorite had a harsh look in her eye, and her face was impassive.

"That's enough!" she said. "I refuse to arrive late for the king's supper just because a village idiot got in my way! Get back here, coachman, and don't spare the horses!"

The marquise was fuming. Her orders couldn't be disobeyed.

"Give that woman ten ecus," she commanded Claude

des Œillets, nodding in the direction of the young man's mother. "And let's be done with it!"

*The price of an infant! A human being's life is cheap as far as she's concerned,* thought Marion, staring at the favorite.

How heartless could this woman be? That radiant smile, those azure eyes, that gentle face—were they just a mask for cruelty and ignominy? Was this the woman the king loved so much that there was nothing he wouldn't do for her?

Athénaïs's reputation as an unscrupulous schemer was only half the story. Whatever people said about her, they greatly underestimated the truth. The Marquise de Montespan was the worst kind of monster. A blood-thirsty beast! And she strutted about freely in sumptuous palaces and gardens, spent vast sums without blinking, and enjoyed the most exquisite meals while prisoners were rotting in humid dungeons and eating moldy bread because they had stolen a couple of apples?

Faced with the marquise's lies about her perfumes, Marion had felt deeply hurt and utterly powerless. Her only recourse, she thought, was to confide her misery to the earth of Versailles. What could a simple servant do against the whims of someone who was almost a queen?

Now, upon discovering all the marquise's detestable deeds while at Clagny, she was seething with disgust and anger. What could be done?

After the accident, one thought began to obsess Marion. She didn't yet know how, but sooner or later, she would take revenge.

## 22

Marion set the pen down on the desk. The sun was rising. It was still dark in Monsieur Le Nôtre's small office, and the orangery was deserted.

On returning from Clagny, the marquise had supper with the king in the bath quarters. She had announced that Claude des Œillets would be watching over her that night. So Marion went to her attic room, but she didn't sleep. Tormented by foreboding and the desire for revenge, she wrote down the words that she had learned by heart:

*I request that the king have an even greater fondness for me than in the past and that he marry me as soon as I am widowed and the queen is holding court in the kingdom of heaven.*

The message was clear. The queen and Monsieur de Montespan were going to die to make room for the beautiful and ambitious Athénaïs.

Marion rolled up the little sheet of paper, slipped it inside a bottle, added an orange blossom, and went into the park to bury it. She felt relieved and tried to sort things out in her head.

How was the favorite going to poison poor

Marie-Thérèse? When exactly would she put her plan into action? Marion sensed that something had to be done fast.

What an affront to Athénaïs if her plan failed! What sweet revenge for all the people she held in contempt and humiliated! Marion felt that vengeance was within reach. But how could she carry it out? Gradually, an idea took shape. . . .

The king! The king had to be warned!

## 23

Marion went back to the marquise's quarters. No one had noticed her absence except Lucie.

On this holiday eve, the linen room was bustling with even more activity than usual. The tailor was there, waiting to be received. Everyone was crowding around the mannequin for a look at the marquise's glistening dress. Marion stepped closer and was speechless on seeing the seamstresses' work. She had often admired the aristocratic ladies as they walked around the grounds in their court attire. She also kept a vivid memory of the clothes and jewelry the guests had worn at the royal entertainment of 1668. But this! She had never seen anything like it! It was a dress straight out of a fairy tale. The gown was made entirely of gold. The shimmering fabric was thickly embroidered in different shades of gold. The lace and ribbons were also gold. And the marquise would certainly wear many large diamonds to add to her splendor.

*A venomous snake dressed in blazing light,* thought Marion. *Well, everything is ready for her triumph over the poor Marie-Thérèse! Perhaps this is a sign. Could the poisoning be imminent?*

Earlier, on the grounds, she had already had a presentiment of impending danger. The king definitely had to be informed of this plot as soon as possible.

Marion knew she wouldn't be allowed to get near the sovereign. She could write him a note, of course, but by the time he read it, it would probably be too late. After careful thought, she came to the conclusion that there was only one person who was close enough to the king to intervene.

She went up to her room, took the flask with her potion out of the small closet, and dabbed a drop under each nostril. Then she immediately left the marquise's quarters.

## 24

"What kind of tall tale is this?" said d'Aquin after Marion had told him everything she knew. "Do you mean to tell me that you can read? First of all, what's your name?"

The physician paced up and down the room as he listened to her. Marion explained to him the same thing she had explained to the marquise. As always when she talked about her mother, her slim fingers reached for the small medallion she wore around her neck.

"It's extremely unusual and commendable for a girl of your station to know how to read and write," d'Aquin said. "Therefore, you're not a fool. You must realize that I can't go to the king and accuse Madame de Montespan. Especially without proof! I think I already told you, incriminating the powerful of this world is out of the question. Do you want me to end my days in the Bastille prison?"

The physician lifted his wig and scratched his head; then he started pacing again like a lion in a cage. Marion watched him. In spite of his grumpy air, made worse by his thick, bushy eyebrows, this man inspired confidence.

Admittedly, his clothes were a bit dirty, but that was often the case at the court. Marion also looked at his shoes, but not a trace of blood was left. She nevertheless congratulated herself on having used her potion. It had at least spared her the fetid odors of the château's many hallways and stairways.

"If you only had one item of proof, just one, of what you're claiming," said d'Aquin.

"I have only the message, monsieur. But I could recognize the smell of the powder, even a pinch of it in a big dish of ragout."

"How do I know you didn't make up the message? And how could you possibly distinguish an odor if it were so diluted?"

"I'm one of the marquise's busy girls. My job consists in watching over her sleep, and—"

"Oh, the marquise's busy girls!" the physician cut her off, laughing. "And how do you spend your time during those long sleepless nights?"

"I create perfumes the marquise asks me to make for her . . . or for others."

"You don't say! A perfumer," replied d'Aquin, suddenly suspicious.

"Not in your meaning of the word, monsieur!" exclaimed Marion indignantly. "I'm not like those charlatans who work for sorcerers. I make real perfumes! I know how to recognize all smells, of every kind."

D'Aquin was troubled by the serious look in Marion's eye and the perfectly sincere expression on her face.

"You've put me in quite a predicament. The queen's life is too precious, so I can't take the risk of not believing you. Tell me about this powder you smelled in Clagny. If it contained poison, can you tell me which one?"

"No, monsieur."

"I thought you could recognize any odor?"

"Yes, but only if I've already smelled it at least once, and I've never smelled poison. The only component of this powder that I could recognize was blood. The rest was foreign to me."

"You see," said d'Aquin as he started to pace around the room again, "sorcerers all do things the same way. Their preparations always contain dried blood taken from the infant victims of their black masses, as well as ashes of their entrails. It's not surprising that you've never smelled any of this."

"Monsieur, isn't there a way we could prevent the black mass planned for tonight and spare the life of an innocent child?"

The physician stopped in front of her. He got down on one knee and spoke softly.

"My poor child, you're so naïve! In the lower depths of Paris, it's easy to find poverty-stricken women for whom a child is just one more mouth to feed. Some women are ready to give up a baby for a few coins. The sorcerers know this and help the women get rid of them. So what will be, will be; tonight or tomorrow, it makes no difference! In our day, motherly love isn't really in style. The police do their job, but unfortunately they can't be everywhere." He stood up. "Let's get back to that powder. . . . Before talking to the king, I have to know for sure whether it really contains poison. I think I have an idea. You'll go back to work at the marquise's and behave completely naturally."

D'Aquin went to a small cupboard and opened its doors, which squeaked very loudly. Inside were bottles of all sizes, boxes, and bundles of paper. He turned to Marion and handed her a flask.

"If you're chosen to watch over your mistress tomorrow night, find a way of adding a few drops of this to her drink. Then open your ears. It is very likely that her tongue will loosen up again during her sleep."

Marion smiled. "And this time, it won't be from indigestion!"

"I see we've understood each other," said d'Aquin. "Go on, and come back to see me tomorrow morning. I hope we'll know more then!"

## 25

The following day was exhausting. The marquise received many people of all sorts in anticipation of the festivities. The tailor and the hairdresser, the shoemaker for the fitting of golden shoes to match her dress, and even Monsieur Le Nôtre, whom the king had asked to confer with the marquise on how to decorate the grove where the refreshments were to be served. This flurry of activity had made Pyrrhos more aggressive than ever. He ended up biting a young seamstress who hadn't been on her guard.

Marion had dreamed of being in on all the little secrets behind the preparations for the celebration. And she was. But some of these secrets were burdensome and might turn out to be dangerous. Marion waited impatiently for evening to come. She was eager to hear the favorite's revelations under the influence of the potion.

Occasionally she glanced out the windows of the formal drawing room. Orange trees in wooden boxes had just been brought in to decorate the marble courtyard. A performance of the tragedy *Alceste* was to be given there the following evening, after the light refreshment. Among the topiaries, she recognized the tiny orange trees she had admired in the orangery. They were her father's creations, and Marion took great pride in them. Each was planted in a porcelain pot and stood on a golden pedestal. A double row of candles was being installed along the roofs, the windows, and the balconies. On the following day, baskets of flowers would be placed at the foot of the orange trees, as well as silver and crystal candelabra.

Finally, at dusk, Marion managed to sleep for an hour. When she woke up, Lucie told her that she had been selected to watch over Athénaïs.

Marion noticed that her friend seemed sad. "What's wrong, Lucie?"

"Martin and I have decided to get married," said Lucie. "He requested permission from the marquise, as required, but she refused. I wanted to discuss it with Mademoiselle des Œillets and ask her to plead in our favor, but I can't find her anywhere. A lackey told me he saw her leave in a carriage an hour ago."

"The marquise is a viper!" exclaimed Marion. The lady-in-waiting was obviously replacing the favorite at the black mass.

Lucie was startled. "What's gotten into you?"

"She's a snake, believe me. I can't tell you more, Lucie. Don't mention anything to anyone, and don't lose heart."

When it was time for the marquise to retire for the night, everything happened exactly as d'Aquin had predicted. Before slipping between the sheets of her large bed, Athénaïs drank a glass of water flavored with orange blossom, which Marion had dosed with the physician's potion. She fell into a deep sleep very quickly, and her nocturnal chatter began almost immediately. The chatter soon turned into ravings, and Marion worried she might have given the marquise too much of the potion.

For this night watch, the favorite had assigned her the task of making the most marvelous perfume she could to further enhance the glamour of the golden dress.

As she worked, Marion didn't miss a single word uttered by the marquise, no matter how muddled she sounded.

This time, Athénaïs carried on about crushing the young mollusk at the appropriate time, sewing the veil around the skeleton, the last feast of the blond curls, and the skull and crossbones of the Gascon.

If the queen's life had not been in danger, Marion would have laughed over what she heard. It didn't make much sense to her. When she reported Athénaïs's ramblings to Monsieur d'Aquin, he would surely be disappointed too.

◦◦◦◦◦

In the morning, Marion left the marquise as soon as the chambermaids came for her *lever*. She went to her room to freshen up and drink a bowl of broth. It was very early, but Lucie had already brought some back from the kitchen. Before running over to the physician's, Marion took out her flask of potion, looked at it thoughtfully, and then put it back in the little closet. She dreaded the odors that had settled in the palace hallways and stairways under cover of darkness, but she might very well need her nose. . . .

The sky was clear and the air very mild. It looked as if Wednesday, July 4, 1674, would be a beautiful day.

## 26

"**I** get it!" d'Aquin cried out. "This is graver than we thought! Two murders aren't enough for her! She's plotting a third!"

The physician had obviously gotten up only a short time before. He was still in his nightgown, which he had quickly tucked into his trousers. Shaggy-haired without his wig, as on the night Marion had first seen him, he was sitting at his desk, cradling his head in his hands.

Marion waited, impatient to hear his conclusions.

"Let's see," he said. "The skull and crossbones represent death, and let me remind you that Monsieur de Montespan is from Gascony. So that confirms the marquise's intentions with regard to her husband! The skeleton is the poor la Vallière, the former favorite. The king criticized her for her thinness a long time before she cloistered herself. The veil sewn around her probably means that the marquise wants her to end her days in the convent."

"What about the mollusk?"

"I'm afraid that's a reference to the dauphin. At

thirteen, he's a fat, slow boy who speaks very little and stuffs himself with sweets all day long." D'Aquin was becoming agitated. "The marquise wants to marry the king, but that's not all she wants. She hopes that one of her sons will inherit the throne of France. For that to happen, the dauphin must die! The queen, the dauphin, and the Marquis de Montespan—that's three murders!"

"So the blond curls are a reference to the queen," added Marion.

"Exactly! What worries me is that last feast the marquise mentioned." After a moment's thought, the physician exclaimed, "And what if it was the banquet planned for tonight, after the performance? I can't see any other explanation!"

Marion shuddered. Her feeling of urgency was becoming fully justified.

"We must act fast!" shouted d'Aquin as he stood up.

He went into his chamber and within a few minutes reappeared fully dressed, holding a small metal box.

"Sit here," he said to Marion, pulling up a chair next to the desk. "I managed to get some samples of the poisons sorcerers use most. You'll smell each one. If the powder meant for the queen is among them, you'll be able to recognize it."

Marion nodded. "I'll certainly recognize it, monsieur," she said confidently.

She congratulated herself for not having used her potion as, one after the other, she sniffed each of the flasks the physician handed to her.

When she smelled the second to last, she threw her head back.

"That's the one!" she shouted. "There's no doubt about it. Other ingredients that are foreign to me have been added. But I would recognize this horrendous odor anywhere!"

D'Aquin sealed the flask and put it back in the box with the others.

"It's a slow-acting poison. A hellish mixture," he said. "The victim doesn't stand a chance of surviving. A drop the size of a pinpoint will kill an infant instantly, while an adult can waste away for a week before dying. Everything lies in the proportions, the size of the victim relative to the quantity of ingested poison. I'll go warn the king at once. But first, I'll take you to the service rooms. Since yesterday, every roasting cook and kitchen boy in the château is working there preparing the banquet. You'll be in charge of sniffing all the dishes going to Her Majesty's table."

Marion was speechless. As of this moment, the life of the queen of France was in her hands.

## 27

The hurried activity in the king's kitchens was beyond description. Marion had no sooner arrived than she was surrounded by the clatter of utensils and the noise of cooks scrambling and shouting nonstop. The heat from the huge chimneys was unbearable. The combined smells of spices, animal carcasses steeped in broth, reheated fat, burnt sauces, peelings, and dishwater turned her stomach. If her assigned mission hadn't been of the utmost importance, she would have fled.

D'Aquin introduced her to an officer. Though the man didn't fully understand why Marion was there, he showed her around the entire kitchen area, room by room. As for the physician, he headed straight for the king's bedchamber. It was time for him to see to his royal patient.

In the course of the day, Marion went through all the rooms smelling the marinades, ragouts, fricassées, sauces, and purées. In the large room where the dishes for the feast were brought in once they were ready, Marion sniffed all the pâtés and pies. She lingered over the pastries, where her nose was relieved to find the delicate perfumes of jam, marzipan, compotes, and cakes of all kinds. She diligently inspected every macaroon. She also went to the larder to check on the cheeses, fruits, and vegetables. As for the dishes from the rotisserie, she planned to attend to them at the last moment.

~∽∽∽∾∾~

Martin came to see her often and brought her things to nibble on. He had tried to find out the reason for her presence in the kitchens, but she remained silent.

D'Aquin joined her at around six in the evening, while the king and his guests waited for light refreshment to be served in the grove.

"I didn't find anything, monsieur," Marion said to him in an undertone. "I'm sorry. No trace of poison at all."

"Keep looking. It may not be too late. I'm going back to my quarters. Keep me informed if there's anything new."

The kitchen frenzy had reached its peak. In only a few hours the king and his guests would have to be served. Marion was walking from one room to another, passing by the pastries, when she noticed two small orange trees on a sideboard. Their leaves were decorated with sweets. She hadn't noticed the trees when she had walked by five minutes earlier.

"These have just been placed here," confirmed a kitchen urchin as he struggled to lift a big cast-iron pot.

"Who brought them in?" asked Marion.

"I don't know," replied the boy, who looked about ten years old. "Ask the big fellow over there." He pointed with his chin to Martin.

Marion immediately went to speak to Martin.

"Those orange trees are for the king and queen. They're beautiful, aren't they?" said Martin. "His Majesty requested they be placed on their table, so they can each easily reach for their favorite sweets. The guests will be served pyramids of sweetmeats on porcelain dishes."

Marion grew alarmed. "Did you see who brought them in?" she asked.

"A young kitchen boy, I think. But I can't tell you his name. On a day like today, we hire anyone who shows up. And I mean anyone!" Martin smiled. "In fact, that lad made us all laugh because he reeked of perfume! Wearing perfume to work in the kitchen! What an absurd idea!"

"What kind of perfume was it?" asked Marion.

Martin shook his head. "I'm not as gifted as you when it comes to these things. It was an unpleasant smell, that's for sure! Just the thing to keep mosquitoes away!"

"Like the smell of geraniums, for example?" pressed Marion.

"That's it," Martin confirmed. "Like the smell of geraniums."

Marion knitted her brows. She knew of only one person who liked essence of geraniums—Claude des Œillets!

She decided to inspect the orange trees more carefully. One was garnished with tiny candied oranges and cherries, as well as fresh strawberries and figs, the king's favorite fruits.

The second had marzipan confections in slightly varying colors. Marion noticed that some had the brown color of chocolate. There was no doubt that this was the tree meant for the queen. Marion got close to the tree, but to her great surprise, she noticed that all the marzipan was odorless! She could smell the earth in the porcelain pot and the wood and foliage, which were so familiar to her. But there was no smell of anything else—no almond, sugar, chocolate, vanilla, or orange blossom. All the aromas that might have delighted her sense of smell were absent. It was completely baffling.

A dreadful suspicion crawled into Marion's mind, followed by a sense of panic. She quickly locked the queen's little orange tree away in a closet, slipped the key into her pocket, and breathlessly darted out of the kitchen.

Lucie was sitting on her bed in their bedroom. She was crying and stuffing herself with cookies Martin had brought her as consolation for their frustrated marriage plans. Without saying a word, Marion opened the closet where she kept her potion. The flask was where it belonged, but it was three-quarters empty. *This morning it was practically full!* she thought.

Everything was becoming clear, but she still had to test one thing. She turned toward Lucie.

"No!" she cried, snatching the last cookie from Lucie's hand just as her friend was going to eat it.

Marion poured two drops of the potion on it and found her suspicions confirmed: the cookie became completely odorless. The potion also worked on matter!

Marion shut her eyes and let out a sigh of despair. She realized how wrong she had been to reveal her secret to the marquise in the gardens of the Trianon, and she finally understood the meaning of the looks exchanged between Athénaïs and Claude des Œillets.

"That viper of a marquise sent someone to rummage through my things," she said to a startled Lucie. "I'm sure she used my potion to conceal the smell of the poison!" Marion swore to herself that from that day on, she would never let anyone in on her secrets.

Now she had to find d'Aquin! Perhaps he would have time to talk to the king again before the supper. She ran off.

## 28

There was the sound of enthusiastic applause. Louis XIV and Queen Marie-Thérèse, the dauphin, and the entire court were acclaiming the musicians and actors of the Royal Academy of Music. Quinault and Lully, the librettist and the composer of the work performed, had just mounted the steps between the royal and marble courtyards and were taking their bows before the aristocratic audience.

After telling d'Aquin all she knew, Marion had returned to her bedroom. At around eight o'clock, she had heard music. The performance was starting. A bit later, the physician had taken her to the royal apartments so they could look down on the scene from a first-floor window.

They saw the king and queen enter the château to go to the banquet hall, where the tables had been set. It was midnight.

"Let's go!" whispered d'Aquin. "I know a spot where we can watch everything without being seen."

As Marion walked next to the physician, she looked at the décor of the rooms. It was imposing, and even more luxurious than the marquise's quarters! All the courtiers had been invited by the king, so along the way the two accomplices met only groups of servants in livery. Some of them greeted the king's head physician and stared with astonishment at the little servant girl who was with him.

D'Aquin, who knew the palace like the back of his hand, opened a door that was concealed behind drapes. He and Marion went down a hallway and reached a kind of windowless alcove, poorly lit by a chandelier with only three candles. The only furnishings consisted of two armchairs, a small round table, and a chest of drawers on which two orange trees had been placed. From an unobtrusive peephole, they could see the banquet hall.

"Their Majesties' table is in the foreground," said d'Aquin in a low voice. Then he stepped away so that Marion could look, standing on her tiptoes. Almost forgetting the danger threatening the queen, she trembled with joy. It made her ecstatic to think that she was in the heart of the Château de Versailles, in one of its most secret hideaways.

The royal couple arrived shortly thereafter, followed by the guests who had been invited to sit at their table.

There was the king's brother and his wife, the stout Princess Palatine. Then came the dauphin, Madame de Montespan, and some ladies of the high nobility whom Louis XIV wanted to honor.

The violinists began to play. They would continue until the end of the meal.

Her eye against the peephole, Marion could not stop admiring all the beautiful dresses with their sparkling colors. The warm, subtle, golden glow from the candles in the candelabra and crystal chandeliers highlighted the brightness of the fabrics and jewelry.

Athénaïs de Montespan, in her golden dress, was without doubt the most beautiful woman there. The poor queen, wearing all the gems in her possession and squeezed into a dreadfully tight corset, glanced enviously at her.

D'Aquin went out to the hall to take a look around.

"The marquise got the king's permission to bring Pyrrhos, while the queen was ordered to leave her dogs in her quarters," he said when he returned. He sighed and sat down. "Now we must wait."

The supper lasted a long time. Marion saw a constant stream of servers bring in dozens of dishes. It was a ballet of sorts, and very pleasant to watch. She could hear the tinkling of the glasses, and the guests' laughter and exclamations. All the marvelous smells reached her nostrils once again.

After the soups, the medium and large entrées, the

highly seasoned dishes, the roasts, the salads, and the salty and sweet dishes, it was finally time for the fruit course.

"Monsieur, they're bringing in the desserts!" whispered Marion, momentarily looking away from the peephole.

"This is it!" said d'Aquin as he jumped up. "Stay here. I'll come back to fetch you very soon."

With those words, the physician tucked an orange tree under each arm and vanished down the hallway.

Meanwhile, on the other side of the partition, the king's table was gradually being laid with pyramids of fresh fruit, large plates with various cakes, brandied fruits, cups of sherbet, bowls of stewed fruit, huge baskets of candied fruit, and countless numbers of small dishes filled with caramels, sugared almonds, and other appetizing sweets. Two small orange trees were also brought in. Marion recognized them immediately. The gentlemen serving the sovereigns set the trees down gently in front of the royal couple. Marion gave a start: the tree with the queen's marzipan was placed in front of the king. As for the queen, she winced upon seeing the tree decked with her husband's favorite fruit placed in front of her.

While conversing with his brother, the king had selected a chocolate marzipan and was holding it in his fingers as he finished his conversation.

The marquise looked petrified. She was as white as a sheet, and though she desperately tried not to show any fear, her eyes betrayed her. Marion almost thought the favorite had stopped breathing.

But Marion knew that even though the favorite resented the king for not renouncing the queen to marry her, she had no wish to harm him. If the king were to die, the marquise would have no status at the court, except as the mother of three illegitimate children. And Queen Marie-Thérèse would assuredly take dreadful revenge on her. In such circumstances, the queen, as regent, would have the power to send the dethroned favorite to a provincial convent for the rest of her life.

Pyrrhos, attracted by the smell of the sweets, started yelping and running around the table. Though he was ignored by everyone, Marion saw him get close to Louis XIV, sit up on his hind legs, and beg. Licking his chops, he started pawing the king's beautiful gem-studded suit.

When he stopped talking to his brother, the king smiled at his wife. He brought the marzipan to his lips, but at the last moment threw it up in the air. Marion heaved a sigh of relief. Then, so as not to miss the astounding sight that was taking place before her eyes, she squashed her nose against the wall. Pyrrhos jumped as high as he could, caught the coveted sweet in midair, and swallowed it in one gulp. That spectacular leap attracted the guests' attention. One minute later, Pyrrhos was shaking with such dreadful convulsions that his body heaved up and down off the ground. In mere seconds, foaming at the mouth and with his eyes rolled upward, he dropped dead on the parquet floor in front of the dumbfounded courtiers.

"His Majesty is expecting you, Marion!" said d'Aquin, smiling.

Marion accompanied him for the second time through the string of antechambers and drawing rooms in the royal apartment. The atmosphere was completely different from that of the previous evening. There were many courtiers waiting to see the king to solicit a favor or pay court to him. A few heads turned as the two went by. Some courtiers smiled mockingly as they watched a little servant girl hurry behind the physician.

That day, Marion was wearing freshly laundered and ironed clothes. Lucie had given her a pretty ribbon she had found after the tailor's visit, and Marion had attached her medallion to it. Her hair was combed neatly back and swept under her embroidered bonnet. Her pretty eyes sparkled with happiness.

When they reached a double door with Swiss guards posted on either side, d'Aquin leaned down and whispered in her ear.

"The king has been informed of the entire affair," he

said. "In fact, last night, as you saw, his plan worked flaw-lessly. He knows, though, that you're the one who saved the queen, thanks to your superior sense of smell. But you must never accuse the marquise. His Majesty doesn't want the mother of several of his children to be implicated in such a sordid poisoning plot without proof. But put your mind at rest. Madame de Montespan has gotten the message, and in the future she'll behave."

The physician had just barely straightened when the door opened.

The king and the queen were sitting in large arm-chairs at the other end of the private drawing room. Marion went up to them slowly and curtseyed awk-wardly.

"Kindly stand up," the king said gently.

Marion couldn't believe her ears. The king of France was treating her with respect.

"Mademoiselle, I will always be grateful to you for what you did for the queen. Monsieur d'Aquin assures me that it's thanks to your remarkable gift for scents that you were able to carry out this feat. I don't mean to put you through another test, but could you tell me which essences went into the perfume I'm wearing?"

Marion had recognized the perfume as soon as she had entered the drawing room. Far from being flustered, she gave the king a very detailed breakdown of its contents and took the liberty of adding, "Your Majesty, I deserve no credit for describing this cologne, since I myself made it at Madame de Montespan's request. She wanted to give it to you as a gift."

Marion glanced at the physician, who was standing off to the side. He had warned her not to implicate the marquise in the poisoning attempt, but he hadn't told her not to mention the favorite in connection with the perfumes.

The king frowned slightly. "I think I recognize you, mademoiselle. I've seen you several times at the marquise's and at the Trianon de Porcelaine. I've been told by several informants that they've often seen a girl who looks like you in the gardens burying something at the foot of trees. Bottles, it seems. Is that indeed you?"

And here Marion had thought that no one knew her secret!

"Yes, Your Majesty," she replied, lowering her eyes.

She then explained when and why she had first developed this habit.

"So you also know how to read and write," the king marveled. "You really are a surprising young person. Now that I'm getting to know you, I don't mind that you're turning my grounds into your secret garden. In fact, I encourage you to continue!"

Queen Marie-Thérèse, surrounded by at least a dozen tiny dogs, looked at Marion and smiled. The king nodded to the queen, and turning back to Marion said, "To show her gratitude, the queen invites you to accompany us on our drive. A barouche is waiting downstairs. It will take us to a place I'm sure you will like."

Marion and d'Aquin followed the sovereigns, and all four climbed into a magnificent barouche under the courtiers' incredulous gazes.

"Forward!" the king shouted to the coachman.

It was splendid weather. The barouche went down the large paths edged with meticulously pruned trees and magnificent flowerbeds. It skirted several ornamental lakes with gigantic fountains whose golden statues were sprayed with a shower of fine, crystalline drops.

Marion was fascinated by this sight and by the king's voice, for he himself commented on all these marvels. When the carriage stopped in front of the grand canal, Marion noticed that two golden gondolas were ready to sail.

Would her dream be fulfilled? She didn't dare believe it until the king invited her to come aboard with him and the queen. Happier than she had ever thought she could be, she let herself be carried along by the waves. What a marvelous gift!

The king had a reputation for fairness. He punished

harshly when it was necessary, but he knew how to reward those who deserved it. Marion now had proof of this. As she fondled her medallion, she was sad that her mother couldn't share this moment of immense joy with her. But she vowed to herself that as soon as the excursion ended, she would run to the orangery to tell her father all about this fairy tale come true. And then, since the sovereign had urged her to keep up her habit, she would also go and confide her happiness to the earth of Versailles.

Slowly, the Venetian gondolier turned the small craft down the right arm of the canal in a northerly direction.

Marion was filled with wonder. Everything was so exquisite! Lulled by the gentle lapping of the water and the king's violins, she admired the flowery lawns and the trees and statues that filed past on each side of the canal. A bit farther ahead, the gardens of the Trianon de Porcelaine were becoming visible in all their splendor.

To her great surprise, Marion saw her father among the crowd of gardeners standing with Augustine and Gaspard Lebon at the top of the stairway leading from the canal to the Trianon flowerbeds. As they cheered, the small group in the gondolas headed for the cabinet of perfumes.

"Please feel at home here," said the king to Marion. "Come whenever you please and stay as long as you wish."

He opened the door to the pavilion himself, then handed her a pretty golden key.

Marion couldn't believe her eyes.

"I—I don't know—what to say. This is too great an honor, Your Majesty. How—how can I thank you?" she stammered.

"Please don't thank me. This isn't a gift, it's a tool to help you fulfill your new duties. The queen will tell you what these duties are."

The queen smiled and spoke for the first time. "You now belong to my household, mademoiselle," she said in a singsong voice that bore a strong Spanish accent.

"Not as a servant, of course. Your talent deserves better. The king has given his consent: from this moment on, you will be my official perfumer."

The queen's perfumer! This was truly the happiest day of Marion's life!

"Thank you so much, Your Majesty," she said, kneeling.

The queen smiled again. "Stand up, mademoiselle," she said kindly. "I have another surprise for you."

∽∽∾∿∾∽

In the company of the king, Monsieur d'Aquin, and all the gardeners, Marion and the queen walked toward the plantations of orange trees on the beautiful, sunny terrace facing south.

"If you hadn't been present, I might have died last night," said Marie-Thérèse. "To commemorate this victory over fate and over my enemies, whoever they may be, I've decided to plant a young orange tree. I hope to live as long as it does!"

"We'll call it the queen's tree," added the king, "to wish it and the queen a long life. And as a way of respecting your mysterious rite, a bottle containing a message of prosperity will be buried at its foot."

Gardeners stepped forward carrying a young shoot and planted it in the ground. A servant brought the queen a bottle. She took a small roll of paper out of her purse and slipped it into the neck of the bottle.

Marion glanced around her quickly. She would have

liked to pick an orange blossom to add to the message as she usually did. Then she changed her mind, for it occurred to her that the queen's tree deserved better than a simple flower. She decided to contribute her most precious possession—her small medallion of the Virgin Mary.

Upon seeing her gesture, the king placed his ring-covered hand on Marion's shoulder.

"Keep that jewel, mademoiselle! Something tells me it means a lot to you," he said.

He himself retied the ribbon Marion had just untied and added a gold coin to the bottle as a symbol of the medallion.

Once the bottle was buried, everyone walked to the grove for refreshments. The king congratulated Marion's father and drank to the health of all the gardeners.

The sun was beginning to set as Marion boarded the gondola to return to the château. This time she was alone with the king; the queen and Monsieur d'Aquin were together in the second gondola.

The king began speaking as soon as they left the landing platform.

"Where did you get the medallion that you were prepared to sacrifice?" he asked.

"It belonged to my mother, Marie," Marion answered. "I received it after her death four years ago."

"How did she come by it?"

"I don't know, sire."

"Well, I'll tell you, because I know that medallion. And I also knew your mother."

Marion gave a start, clasped the medallion, and looked straight into the king's eyes.

"This was when we were children. She was the daughter of one of the servants of my mother, Queen Anne. I was seven and she was six. We were always together, even when my tutors came to teach me French. That's how she learned to read. She had a very lively mind, and while pretending to play with her dolls, she didn't miss a single word of what was being said. Afterward, as soon as we were alone, I would teach her to write her letters and I would correct her mistakes. I was extremely fond of Marie," added the king with a sigh. "You might even say she was my first true love. Would you believe me if I told you I had all kinds of little nicknames for her? 'My queen' was the one she liked best, and in the end that was what I called her! 'My queen' suited her well, she was so pretty. . . . One day, I decided to offer her a gift as a token of my friendship; I asked my mother to give me something from her jewelry box. At first she refused, but I was so insistent that she finally relented and gave me that medallion. My dear Marie always wore it from that day on."

"As I do now, since she passed away," murmured Marion.

"Later on," the king continued, "life separated us, as

you might have guessed. I never saw Marie again. Please tell me, mademoiselle, what your mother died of?"

"She died bathed in blood because of a midwife who was completely drunk, the only one my father could find in the middle of the night. Augustine Lebon was taking care of me, but I escaped her and saw what I was not supposed to see. Ever since then, I don't sleep well. I can't bear the sight of blood, and even worse to me is its odor."

"Poor child!" said the king softly as he saw the tears roll down Marion's cheeks.

He handed her a pretty, lace-trimmed handkerchief. As Marion brought it to her face, she smelled the perfume she had unknowingly created for him not so long ago. It was a marvelous scent. She inhaled it deeply, and little by little her sorrow dissipated.

"I'm sorry. I didn't mean to make such lovely eyes cry," the king said. He cleared his throat before continuing. "You know, mademoiselle, I still have the strange childhood habit of giving everyone nicknames. Well, I've found one that suits you perfectly." When he saw Marion's stunned expression, the king asked, "Wouldn't you like to know what it is?"

"Yes I would, Your Majesty."

"Your mother was 'My queen.' From now on, I'll call you 'My princess.' Isn't the daughter of a queen always a princess?"

Marion and the king looked at each other and burst out laughing.

❧⟳❧

That evening, in her new lodgings one flight above Queen Marie-Thérèse's quarters, Marion climbed into a soft, cozy bed and slept through the night for the first time in four years.

# ❧ Epilogue ❧

The king did not want to distress Athénaïs, the beautiful marquise. He ordered no inquiry into the poisoning, thinking he had settled the matter on his own. Yet Madame de Montespan continued to consult astrologers, fortune-tellers, and sorcerers of all kinds.

Thereafter, she did not stay in favor very long. In 1679, the notorious Poison Affair was exposed. The favorite was implicated in a number of poisoning cases, and the king turned away from her for good.

Claude des Œillets, her first lady-in-waiting, confidante, and companion, was also involved. She had merely obeyed her mistress's orders; however, she was cruelly punished. Interned by order of the king in a squalid hospice in the provinces, she died there in 1686, abandoned by all.

Queen Marie-Thérèse, on the other hand, savored her victory over life and over her rival. This short, plump Spanish infanta with bad teeth was a fair-minded, attentive, and humane woman who was passionately fond of children. She hadn't been lucky with her own. By the time she met Marion, the only one who was still alive was the dauphin. Marie-Thérèse had been particularly affected by the death of her last daughter, aged five. When she first saw Marion, she thought the young girl bore a strange resemblance to her deceased daughter and immediately took her under her wing.

After that July day in 1674, the queen returned to her old routines. She continued to say her prayers, play with her dwarf jesters, and stuff herself with chocolate. In short, nothing much had changed in her life. Nothing except the presence of Marion, whom she sincerely loved, just as she loved the sumptuous, unique perfumes the young girl created for her delight.

~∞∞∞~

Shortly after Marion entered the queen's service, Lucie Cochois and Martin Taillepierre were granted the king's approval to marry. The young cook continued to work in the royal kitchens, where his talent was soon recognized. To her great joy, Lucie left the marquise's staff as well and joined the queen's service.

When Marie-Thérèse died in July 1683, Marion became the Sun King's perfumer.

Antoine Dutilleul was very proud of his daughter. Augustine and Gaspard Lebon and all the gardeners who had seen Marion grow up shared his sentiment.

Ever since, whenever the gardeners planted a tree on the grounds of the château, they buried a bottle beneath it containing a message of prosperity for the tree and wishing it a long life. And they added a small gold coin as a symbol of the medallion of Mary.

By using this marvelous story to create a tradition, the gardeners found their own way of paying a moving tribute to Marion's extraordinary destiny and to her passion for the fragrances, the earth, and the blossoms of the orange trees of Versailles.

# Author's Note

## PERFUMES IN THE AGE OF THE SUN KING

At Versailles in the seventeenth century, as everywhere in France and across Europe, people were afraid of water. Why? Because water, they believed, carried the miasmas of the plague. (The germ theory of disease did not exist at the time.) The devastating effects of the Black Death, the bubonic plague of 1348, had not been forgotten.

Because of this fear, instead of washing with water, people washed with perfumed substances. It is commonly said that in the age of Louis XIV people never washed at all and that they masked their bad body odors by dousing themselves with perfume. This is partly true, but the situation was much more complicated. In fact, in those days, perfume was believed to have a wide range of properties and functions.

*A social function:* Perfume was a luxury. Only wealthy people could afford to buy it, use it—and overuse it. So perfume was their way of asserting their personality and flaunting their social rank.

*A hygienic function:* Since water was excluded from the routines of personal hygiene, people washed with small pieces of cloth soaked in perfumed substances, or "toilet vinegar"; they washed their hands in spirits of wine; they chewed lozenges containing spices to clean their teeth and freshen their breath; they softened and whitened their hands using bars of almond soap and iris paste.

Let us remember that the period we are talking about was three centuries ago! In those days people did not have the same notions of hygiene as they do today. Fleas, lice, and other vermin were not considered dirty; nor were bedbugs.

Everyone had to live with them—including the king. They were a common scourge that each person coped with in his or her own way.

*A protective function:* Perfume was thought to guard against air contaminated by miasmas. Not only did people surround themselves with a halo of perfume, they also hid small sachets of fragrant powder in their clothes and burned scented pastilles in their bedrooms and drawing rooms.

*A therapeutic function:* It was believed that wearing perfume, or breathing the vapors of scented pastilles, was a remedy for a person's ills. According to this view, inhaled aromatic preparations entered the lungs and bloodstream and had a beneficial effect deep inside the body. Perfume was thus regarded as a healing agent, a kind of apothecary's formula. This is why other ingredients were added to the perfume mixture, ingredients that physicians believed, on purely empirical grounds, possessed curative powers. These ingredients included extracts of wolf liver, fox lung, bear fat, and worm oil, as well as gold, silver, and fine pearl powder, and also, occasionally, less appetizing substances, such as blood, urine, and excrement.

Fortunately, in spite of all these uses, the prime function of perfume remained intimately linked to the notion of pleasure.

## The Profession of a "Nose"

As Marion is in *The Orange Trees of Versailles,* a "nose" is a creator of perfumes—someone who blends scents into fragrances.

A nose is often modest about his or her gift. It's common for a nose to claim no more than an ordinary olfactory sense, and to assert that only years of training and tireless work have enabled him or her to map out the blend of a perfume. Just as a painter will make many sketches before ever touching brush to canvas, so a nose will follow the flow of his or her research for weeks, possibly even months. A nose will make changes, enrich the original framework of scents, until he or she obtains the ideal alchemy, the perfect fullness of an original fragrance.

A nose will not mention the extraordinary olfactory memory that allows him or her to recognize 3,500 different scents. And a nose will forget the subtle capacity he or she possesses for imagining a finished perfume.

To say that this is a true gift—indeed a rare and precious one—may go against the legendary modesty of noses, but a gift it is. Noses are unique artists.

## SOME FAMOUS NOSES AND THEIR CREATIONS

### The GUERLAIN Dynasty

| | |
|---|---|
| Pierre-François-Pascal Guerlain | Eau de Cologne Impériale |
| | *Created for Empress Eugénie in 1853* |
| Aimé Guerlain | Jicky (1889) |
| Jacques Guerlain | L'Heure Bleue (1912) |
| | Mitsouko (1919) |
| | Shalimar (1925) |
| Jean-Paul Guerlain | Jardins de Bagatelle (1983) |
| | Samsara (1989) |

### CHRISTIAN DIOR

| | |
|---|---|
| Edmond Roudnitska | Eau Sauvage (1966) |
| Maurice Roger | Poison (1985) |
| | Fahrenheit (1988) |

## CHANEL

| Ernest Beaux | No. 5 (1921) |
| Henri Robert | No. 19 (1970) |
| Jacques Polgex | Coco (1984) |

## LANVIN

| André Fraysse | Arpège (1927) |

## NINA RICCI

| Robert Ricci | L'Air du Temps (1948) |

## ROCHAS

| Edmond Roudnitska | Femme (1944) |
| Nicolas Mamounas | Byzance (1987) |

## PATOU

| Henri Almeras | Joy (1930) |

## TECHNIQUES OF PERFUME MANUFACTURING

Today, thanks to centuries of improvements in manufacturing tools, perfumes are designed with advanced technical knowledge.

In the past, the principal technique was based on the affinity between fatty material and odor. This is the process that Marion uses in the novel. It is called enfleurage and can be executed with or without heat. Cold enfleurage is used primarily with delicate flowers such as jasmine.

A later method was distillation with an alembic, a technique based on steam's potential to extract essential oils. This process is still used today. Indeed, in Provence, it is not unusual to see enormous mobile alembics steaming at the edge of a lavender field, and then to see the alembics moved from field to field. Unfortunately, this method has its limits. Though it produces wonders with lavender, sandalwood, and vetiver, it cannot be applied to all plants.

For mimosa or narcissus, for example, it is necessary to use the method called extraction by volatile solvents. This technique involves treating flowers several times with a solvent until the plant material is depleted. At that point the solvent is steeped with odoriferous substances; the solvent becomes a pasty mixture. This is followed by several different processes—an alcohol treatment, a cold treatment, and evaporation of the alcohol. Finally, a pure product is obtained, the purest of the pure, the one sought after by all perfumers: an absolute.

Lastly, there is the cold expression method, the process used with hesperidia. (A hesperidium is a berry that has a leathery rind, such as orange, lemon, citron, and bergamot.) Cold expression involves pressing the rinds to recover fine droplets composed of water and an aromatic essence.

Having used these methods to obtain the necessary basic products, a nose can proceed to design the blend. Once the nose has established the blend's formula, a concentrate can be manufactured. The next step is maceration: mixing the concentrate with alcohol. (In France, beet alcohol is used because of its neutral odor.) Maceration can take up to three months. The quantity of alcohol used varies according to the type of product desired (from most potent to mildest): *parfum, eau de parfum, eau de Cologne,* or *eau de toilette.* After the perfume is filtered to remove any remaining impurities, it is bottled and, at last, ready to spread the romance, fantasy, sensuality, and magic of its bouquet around the world.